FAVORITES BY CHRIS GRABENSTEIN

Dog Squad
The Island of Dr. Libris
No More Naps!
Shine! (coauthored by J.J. Grabenstein)

THE MR. LEMONCELLO'S LIBRARY SERIES

Escape from Mr. Lemoncello's Library
Mr. Lemoncello's Library Olympics
Mr. Lemoncello's Great Library Race
Mr. Lemoncello's All-Star Breakout Game
Mr. Lemoncello and the Titanium Ticket

THE SMARTEST KID IN THE UNIVERSE SERIES

The Smartest Kid in the Universe
Genius Camp

THE WELCOME TO WONDERLAND SERIES

Home Sweet Motel
Beach Party Surf Monkey
Sandapalooza Shake-Up
Beach Battle Blowout

THE HAUNTED MYSTERY SERIES

The Crossroads
The Demons' Door
The Zombie Awakening
The Black Heart Crypt

COAUTHORED WITH JAMES PATTERSON

The House of Robots series
The I Funny series
The Jackie Ha-Ha series
Katt vs. Dogg
The Max Einstein series
Pottymouth and Stoopid
The Treasure Hunters series
Word of Mouse

THE SMARTEST KID IN THE UNIVERSE

GENIUS CAMP

CHRIS GRABENSTEIN

RANDOM HOUSE 🏠 NEW YORK

Text copyright © 2021 by Chris Grabenstein
Jacket art copyright © 2021 by Antoine Losty

All rights reserved. Published in the United States by
Random House Children's Books, a division of
Penguin Random House LLC, New York.

Random House and the colophon are registered trademarks
of Penguin Random House LLC.

Visit us on the Web! rhcbooks.com

Educators and librarians, for a variety of teaching tools,
visit us at RHTeachersLibrarians.com

Library of Congress Cataloging-in-Publication Data
Name: Grabenstein, Chris, author.
Title: Genius Camp / Chris Grabenstein.
Description: First edition. | New York: Random House, [2021] |
Series: The smartest kid in the universe series; [book 2]
Summary: "Twelve-year-old Jake McQuade—the smartest kid in the universe—
goes to a camp for geniuses, where he goes up against the Virtuoso quantum
computer, the smartest machine in the universe" —Provided by publisher.
Identifiers: LCCN 2021005415 | ISBN 978-0-593-30177-7 (trade) |
ISBN 978-0-593-30178-4 (lib. bdg.) | ISBN 978-0-593-43375-1 (int'l ed.) |
ISBN 978-0-593-30179-1 (ebook)
Subjects: CYAC: Genius—Fiction. | Camps—Fiction. | Computers—Fiction. |
Humorous stories.
Classification: LCC PZ7.G7487 Ge 2021 | DDC [Fic]—dc23

Printed in the United States of America
10 9 8 7 6 5 4 3 2 1
First Edition

For all the scientists who helped us so much in 2020–2021

1

Twelve-year-old Jake McQuade had never flown a military helicopter behind enemy lines, but it really wasn't all that hard.

Sure, bad guys kept firing machine guns and mortars and Hydra rockets at him, but Jake and his chopper dodged all the incoming fire.

"Well done, son!" said the general strapped in beside him.

"Just using my math and geometry skills, sir."

"Now we need to go rescue the hostages!"

Six pulsing green dots throbbed on the holographic display projected on the whirlybird's windshield. They showed Jake the precise location of the hostages: trapped behind the walls of a heavily armed desert fortress the helicopter was heading to.

A nasty new fireball erupted on Jake's right. Another near miss. He jerked the joystick to the left.

"Warning," said the onboard computer. "Fighter jet on your tail. Prepare for missile attack."

"Two can play at that game," said Jake. He punched in a string of code—an algorithm he'd actually written himself—that would command his starboard Sidewinder missile to execute a complex backward, loop-the-loop, boomerang shot that no chopper pilot had ever dared attempt before.

"If the next missile hits us, son, we're toast!" barked the general. "Toast!"

"Hold off on the marmalade, sir!"

Jake punched the launch button.

The rocket streaked away in a blistering plume of white. It arced up and over the helicopter, flipped back around, and surprised the enemy jet with a direct heat-seeking hit to its tailpipe.

BA-BOOM!

"Woo-hoo!" cried Jake, doing a quick arm-chugging, hip-swiveling chair dance.

"Well done!" shouted the general.

"Math and physics, sir. Math and physics."

A two-note danger signal blared.

"Fish sticks!" shouted the general. "That was our final weapon!" More angry warning lights throbbed up and down the control panel. "The bad guys still have rockets, mortars, and a tank!"

"Good," said Jake.

"What?"

"Their tank, sir. We're gonna borrow it!"

Jake tapped another string of code into the chopper's onboard computer. Up until a few months ago, all he could tap were one-finger text messages with lots of emojis so he didn't have to spell so many words. But then, overnight, things changed. Jake McQuade became supersmart.

"I can hack into the enemy's system data through heat emissions, then use the thermal sensors of my computer to transfer command and control of that tank's weaponry to me!"

"But the enemy tank is a T-26-Z—the heaviest ever built. It's stuck in the mud. It's run out of fuel. It can't move."

"Temporary problems, sir. Which, by the way, are way more fun than math problems. Time for a mic drop."

Jake deployed the giant superhydraulic electromagnet positioned underneath his helicopter's belly. The thing was straight out of a scrap metal junkyard. The "Big Grabber" was standard equipment on this, the most sophisticated chopper in the military's secret arsenal. It's why Jake had selected it for this mission.

"It's all tangents and vectors from here, sir. And yaw. Can't forget the yaw. It's in all the flight manuals."

Jake flawlessly executed a deft series of moves. He heard the solid, metallic *THUNK* the instant his heavy-duty magnet snagged the ginormous tank and hoisted it up off the ground. The thing swung from the helicopter like a forty-ton yo-yo.

Jake, of course, still had to evade incoming mortar rounds. And a few more rocket shots. But avoiding those blasts was a simple matter of three-dimensional point-plotting. Finally, at precisely the right moment, and compensating for the arc of the dangling tank's swing, he fired.

The tank's turret gun blasted a hole in the side of the fortress wall.

Jake fired again.

The hole became a tunnel.

Jake swung the tank sideways. With the flick of a switch, he turned off the electromagnet. The T-26-Z flew away and cratered into the desert floor.

Free of the tank's weight, Jake could easily maneuver the helicopter into position for a soft landing.

The six terrified hostages rushed out of the escape tunnel and climbed into the chopper.

"Well done, son!" said the general. "You just set a new world record for *Gunship Air Battle Extreme*!"

Jake heard a buzzer sound. Bells rang. A crowd cheered and chanted his name.

He peeled off his headset and virtual reality goggles.

Up on the giant video screen in the hotel ballroom, his name was at the top of the leaderboard!

2

"The smartest kid in the universe has just defeated the world's smartest computer!" announced the emcee onstage with Jake.

Triumphant *whoop-whoop* music blasted out of concert speakers. Jake waved at the six hundred gamers and fans crammed into the ballroom of the Imperial Marquis, the hotel where his mom was the events coordinator. In Jake's humble opinion, this e-games competition, the first Zinkle Extreme Masters Tournament, was the best event his mom or the hotel had ever hosted.

A dozen hard-core gamers had just gone up against the Zinkle Virtuoso, the smartest, fastest, most artificially intelligent computer ever created by legendary tech whiz Zane Zinkle. That's why there were a dozen names on the leaderboard. But JAKE MCQUADE was all the way up at the top!

"Smart thinking with that tank, Jake!" said Grace Garcia, joining Jake onstage. Grace was another seventh grader at Riverview Middle School. One of the smartest. Definitely the prettiest. At least that's what Jake thought, even though he was too chicken to tell her. "You were amazing!"

"Um, thanks."

Jake's pale, freckled face went code pink. Grace had that effect on him. When she smiled and her eyes sparkled, Jake blushed.

"Who loves ya, baby?" Now his best bud, Kojo Shelton, was on the stage. Kojo was smart and funny and, for whatever reason, loved to stream TV shows from way back in the 1970s and '80s, including one he'd stumbled across called *Kojak*.

"We might be soul mates," he'd once told Jake. "He's Ko-*jak* and I'm Ko-*jo*. Sure, he's a bald, old Greek dude and I'm a handsome, young Black dude, but come on—we both dig Tootsie Pops."

"Who loves ya, baby?" was Kojak's old catchphrase. It had quickly become Kojo's new one.

"I'll tell you who loves him," said Grace. "This whole crowd. Jake, you were fantástico!"

"Gracias," he told her, because he'd recently become fluent in Spanish. The Spanish he learned the old-fashioned way. Studying. The stuff he knew to win the video game? A lot of that came from the jelly beans. The Ingestible Knowledge chewables that only Grace, Kojo,

6

Jake, and their absentminded inventor friend, Haazim Farooqi, knew about.

"What're you going to do with the prize money?" Grace asked.

"Donate it to charity, of course," said Jake.

"Awesome. Pick your charity and I'll match your donation."

Jake might be "the smartest kid in the universe," but Grace Garcia was on the short list for "the richest kid in the world," on account of her family's buried treasure, which the three friends had discovered while working together to save their school. Sure, Grace spent a lot of her money on sneakers (including some very colorful Air Jordans), but she also supported more charities than Jake could count, and he could count pretty high. One of the jelly beans had made him a math whiz.

A slender young man in blue jeans and a black turtleneck snaked his way through the mob crowding the hotel ballroom floor.

The man, who had a security detail clearing the way for him, wore glasses with round, invisible frames and looked like he trimmed his shaggy bangs with a toenail clipper. Jake recognized him immediately. Zane Zinkle. The head of Zinkle Inc., maker of Zinkle computers, zPhones, zPads, zBox gaming systems, and tons of software. Zinkle was also the mind behind Virtuoso—the supersmart quantum computer that Jake had just defeated in the head-to-head video game competition.

Zinkle was the most famous bazillionaire in the high-tech world. He was bigger than any of the brainiacs out in Silicon Valley. And he was only twenty-nine years old.

Zinkle was trailed by a team of eager assistants, all of them dressed in blue jeans and black turtlenecks. One guy was toting a giant cardboard check made out to *Jake McQuade*. A check worth twenty thousand dollars.

"Dag," said Kojo when he saw the check. "You sure you want to give all that money to charity?"

Jake looked to Grace. She smiled.

"I know an animal rescue group that could really use the help," she said. "They find homes for cats and dogs."

"Yeah," said Jake, smiling back. "I'm all in, Kojo."

"Cool. That's what I'd do, too. Especially for, you know, cats and dogs. Love me some cats and dogs."

Zinkle, his security detail, and his staff made their way up onto the stage.

"Congratulations, Mr. McQuade," said Zinkle, adjusting his glasses with his pinky.

"Thank you, sir."

"Would you like to pose with the check now?" asked a woman in his entourage. Her glasses matched Zinkle's.

"Not now, Christina!" Zinkle snapped.

"Of course, not now, sir. I meant later. Whenever it's convenient."

Zinkle turned back to Jake. His smile looked like it hurt his face.

"Jake, you are the first gamer to ever defeat Virtuoso.

We're going to have to analyze what went wrong with its AI this afternoon, aren't we, Christina?"

"Yes, sir. Right away, sir."

Zinkle's smile broadened. "I must say, Jake, your move with the tank was extremely . . . unorthodox."

Jake shrugged. "I improvised. Zigged when Virtuoso probably figured I'd zag."

Jake's little sister, Emma, a nine-year-old fourth grader, squeezed her way through the crowd. Their mom was with her.

"Jake? My friend Avery wants a selfie with you," said Emma. "She's your biggest fan. Don't ask me why. . . ."

"Emma?" said their mom with a laugh. "Be nice."

"I'm just busting his chops a little, Mom. Somebody has to or he'll get a big head."

Jake grinned. "Come on, Emma. Let's go take a selfie with Avery. Catch you later, Mr. Zinkle."

With Emma leading the way, Jake followed his family offstage.

"Sorry you didn't get your picture, Mr. Zinkle," said Grace. She grabbed the giant cardboard check. "Thanks for this."

"If you still want that photo," said Kojo, handing Zinkle a crisp business card, "have your people call Jake's people, which, hello, is me, baby. I am the man's main man."

Kojo and Grace followed Jake.

Zinkle narrowed his eyes as they strode away.

"Christina?"

"Sir?"

"Where's my car?"

"Outside, sir."

"Why is it outside? I need it. Now! Get me out of here!"

"Yes, sir. Right away, sir."

The burly security guards wedged their way through the crowd, plowing a path to the exit.

Zinkle pinky-adjusted his glasses again.

And muttered Jake McQuade's name over and over and over, all the way out to the street.

3

A few days later, Jake, Kojo, and Grace were in the dressing room of a television studio where Jake was about to appear on the hit game show *Quiz Zone*.

"The mayor loves *Quiz Zone*," Grace had told Jake one day during social studies. "If you go on the show and win, I guarantee she'll want to meet you."

"And if she wants to meet you," added Kojo, "she'll need to schedule a meeting with *us* to talk about our recycling project."

So Jake had accepted the invite to do the game show. Now Grace was smearing goop on his face.

"He has to wear makeup?" said Kojo, crinkling his nose.

"It's a TV show," said Grace. "Everybody on TV wears makeup."

"Even the soccer players?"

11

"That's different," said Jake.

"How?" asked Kojo. "I watch soccer on TV. . . ."

"Kojo?" Grace said firmly.

Kojo held up both hands in surrender.

Jake was about to compete against the two all-time *Quiz Zone* champions: college professor Dr. Zelda Melinger and former professional pinochle player Danny Fontaine.

Millions of viewers (including the mayor) would be watching. It was must-see TV: the smartest kid in the universe versus the world's smartest adults.

"You nervous?" asked Grace.

"A little bit," said Jake. His eyes darted around the room to make sure nobody was listening. "What if the you-know-whats wear off in the middle of the show?"

"The jelly beans?" blurted Kojo. "Are those the you-know-whats? Mr. Farooqi's jelly beans?"

"Kojo?" said Grace.

"Sorry. Forgot we were still going incognito about Haazim and his, uh, confectionery creations."

"Mr. Farooqi doesn't want anybody to know about his IK experiments until he can replicate the you-know-whats he gave Jake," Grace reminded Kojo.

"Actually," said Kojo, "he didn't *give* the you-know-whats to you-know-who."

It was true. Jake had found an unmarked jar of jelly beans in what was called the greenroom of his mother's hotel conference center. It was where speakers waited before they went onstage. That night, there'd been a major scientific symposium taking place in the ballroom. Jake was hungry. He saw the jelly beans. They weren't labeled with anybody's name. No one was around to claim them. So he scarfed down the whole jar. Less than half an hour later, he was super intelligent.

A TV tech wearing a headset knocked on the dressing room door. "Ready, Mr. McQuade?"

"Uh, yeah," said Jake. "I guess."

"Great. Let's head out to the set."

"Good luck!" said Grace.

"Just be you," encouraged Kojo. "The new, smart you. Not the old, lazy you."

Jake followed his escort into the brightly lit studio and waved at his mom and Emma, who were in the front row of the audience bleachers. Grace and Kojo took seats next to them. Jake shook hands with his competitors, Dr. Melinger and Mr. Fontaine.

"Good luck, kid," said Dr. Melinger, the college professor.

"You're definitely going to need it," sniped Mr. Fontaine, the pinochle player. Both returning champions had smug sneers on their faces. Jake was a cockroach, and they were the shoes about to squish him.

"Don't let them get inside your head!" coached Grace from the bleachers. "It's already crowded enough in there."

The game show's theme music started up. The studio

audience applauded. The famous host strode to his desk to introduce the contestants. Jake had to stand on a wooden box. He was too short for his podium.

"Here's our first *Quiz Zone* question," said the host. "Contestants, please buzz in if you know the answer—but kindly wait until after I finish reading the entire question."

Jake fidgeted with his buzzer button. His hands were sweaty. He knew sweat glands were particularly numerous on your palms and under your armpits. When you're feeling stressed, nerves activated these sweat glands. When those nerves overreacted, it caused hyperhidrosis.

Jake hoped *hyperhidrosis* would be the answer to the first question.

It wasn't.

The host read the question off a card as it appeared on a studio monitor.

"John's father has five sons: Alan, Blan, Clan, and Dlan. What did he call his fifth son?"

The pinochle champ was the first to buzz in.

"Mr. Fontaine?" said the host.

"Elan," he said confidently. "The five names obviously follow a logical alphabetical progression, *A, B, C, D.* So *E*-lan would be next."

The college professor made a face. She would have given the same answer.

"I'm sorry," said the host. "That is incorrect."

Jake buzzed in.

"Mr. McQuade?"

"Um, the fifth son's name was John. Because in your question you said, 'John's father had five sons.' So one of the sons has to be, you know, named John."

"That is correct!"

Jake's sweat glands calmed down after that.

As the game continued, he beat the two grown-ups to the buzzer and answered every single question correctly.

During a commercial break, Jake, Kojo, and Grace exchanged a triple fist bump.

"You're on fire, baby," said Kojo.

"I feel sorry for the professor and the pinochle player," said Grace. "Which, by the way, sounds like the title of a bad movie."

"You think I should go easy on them?" asked Jake.

"Well, we are given our talents to help others, not ourselves."

"But that rule doesn't apply during TV game shows," insisted Kojo.

Grace laughed. "Kojo's right. Just have fun."

I will, thought Jake. *Because* my *talents could wear off at any second.*

4

Haazim Farooqi was streaming *Quiz Zone* on his phone, taking a break from his top-secret research in the shiny new college lab.

"Way to go, Subject One!" he cheered as Jake fielded question after question correctly. Farooqi was absent-mindedly jiggling a beaker full of bright red liquid while he watched. The cylinder bubbled and steamed. He called Jake "Subject One" because Jake McQuade was the first (and, so far, only) person to eat any of his Ingestible Knowledge capsules.

But, oh, the wonders IK would do for the world, once Haazim replicated his earlier experiment and mass-produced his jelly beans. Easter baskets would never be the same! Nor would anything else. Diseases would be cured. Cars would run on salt water. Lunches would make themselves. The world would be so much better because the world would be so much smarter.

Subject One had been very grateful for his newfound intelligence. He even used his share of the treasure that he and his two friends had discovered to finance Farooqi's biomedical engineering studies at Rutgers University in New Jersey. Soon Haazim would earn his PhD and become Dr. Farooqi. Especially if he could re-create his chewable IK tablets. Especially if they came in delicious flavors, like Buttered Popcorn, Cotton Candy, Watermelon, and Juicy Pear.

Unfortunately, Farooqi had not kept very good notes when he created his miracle pills, and so far, no matter what he tried or tinkered with, he couldn't figure out how to redo what he'd done that first time. He vowed to be more organized. He even bought a day planner. And a notebook with unicorns on the cover.

"All right, Jake," said the game show host on Farooqi's phone screen. His goatee made him look like a dapper professor or a poet. "Get ready for your final, bonus question. That's coming up right after another word from our sponsor—Zinkle Inc.'s all-new zPhone! It's ama-Z-ing!"

Farooqi, whose intense brown eyes looked even more intense when magnified by the wraparound safety goggles he wore at all times (because danger never took a day off), had come to the United States from Pakistan to major in biochemistry with a focus on neurology, the study of the brain. At thirty-three, he was a little older than the much more famous Zane Zinkle. But he was also a genius like Zinkle, even if nobody except his mother realized it. Farooqi's mother. Not Zinkle's.

Quiz Zone came back from its commercial break.

"Welcome back," said the host. "Okay, Jake. Here is your final, bonus question. Get it right, and you'll double your winnings."

The lights dimmed. The music was dramatic.

Farooqi moved his phone closer to his safety goggles.

"In the most recent edition of the *Oxford English Dictionary,* one word is spelled incorrectly."

The studio audience gasped. Farooqi did, too. How dare they call themselves a dictionary if they spelled even one word wrong?

"What is that word?"

The camera cut to a close-up of Jake. He looked confused. Puzzled. His eyebrows were arched high.

"Don't let me down, Subject One!" Farooqi said aloud. "And don't let those people in Oxford get away with their sloppy misspelling!"

Farooqi hoped Jake's jelly bean–fueled brain knew the correct answer. Having his first test subject crush the two grown-up geniuses on *Quiz Zone* would be another feather in his cap, if he ever wore a cap and wasn't allergic to feathers.

Jake shrugged, tossed up his hands, and said, "Um, I'm pretty sure the word that's spelled incorrectly is, you know, 'incorrectly.' There's also a word that's spelled wrong. 'W-R-O-N-G.' "

The camera switched to the game show host.

"That answer is . . ."

He took a long pause to build suspense.

Farooqi moved even closer to his phone.

". . . correct! You've doubled your winnings!"

"Balley balley! Shahbaash!" Farooqi rejoiced with an exuberant soccer-goal-worthy arm pump.

Unfortunately, that gesture jerked up the beaker in his hand and sent its steaming red liquid flying.

Some of the red stuff splashed into an open rack of test tubes filled with burbling blue sludge.

When the steaming red liquid hit the blue glop, purple foam exploded skyward. It splatted on the ceiling. Violet bubbles sizzled across the tiles where the shouldn't-be-mixed-together chemicals burst into multicolored flames, which triggered the lab's sprinkler system.

Farooqi and all his lab gear were drenched by an indoor rainstorm. The water soaked the pages of his notebook and turned his formulas and calculations into splotchy blue ink blobs. His day planner was a papers-stuck-together mess.

Haazim Farooqi's most recent attempt to re-create his Ingestible Knowledge capsules was ruined. All progress had been erased.

But, on the bright side, his shiny new lab did smell like a purple Island Punch Jelly Belly jelly bean—fruity with a tinge of coconut.

At least he'd accomplished that much.

Otherwise, his Ingestible Knowledge research project had just been sent all the way back to square one.

5

Jake learned most of what he knew about Ingestible Knowledge from a TED Talk he'd streamed on his computer.

Dr. Sinclair Blackbridge, a famous futurist from the Massachusetts Institute of Technology, a guy who'd predicted everything from internet shopping to GPS devices in cars (way before anybody else believed in the stuff), had recorded a short lecture titled "Our Brilliant Tomorrow." In it, he predicted what the next big thing would be.

Jake had watched the clip three dozen times.

"For centuries, we humans have consumed information through our eyes and our ears," Dr. Blackbridge told his audience. "But in the not-too-distant future, we are going to ingest information. You're going to swallow a pill and know English. You're going to swallow a pill and know geometry, trigonometry, and quantum physics. You'll take another pill and instantly speak Swahili."

Yep. After eating Mr. Farooqi's jelly beans, Jake had instantly spoken Swahili.

The morning after his *Quiz Zone* appearance, Jake and his jelly-beaned brain bopped down the halls of the recently refurbished Riverview Middle School.

He knocked knuckles with some of his buds. They mostly used the hand that wasn't already busy cradling a smartphone.

"You're awesome on *Quiz Zone,* dude!" said Hargun Singh without looking up from his device. "I'm streaming it again. This is my third time!"

"Hey, Jake!" shouted Latoya Sherron. "Loved that 'wrong' answer last night!"

"Thanks!"

Jake could've spent all morning shooting the breeze with his friends, who included just about every kid at Riverview. But he didn't want to be late for class. One of the first things he'd learned when his brain made its jelly bean–fueled leap? Learning stuff was actually pretty cool.

The school's new principal, Mr. Charley Lyons, a distant relative of Grace Garcia whom she called Uncle Charley, stepped out of his office. He was not gazing at his phone.

"Did you remember your uniform, Mr. McQuade?"

Principal Lyons was also the basketball coach.

"Yes, sir," said Jake. The BJB (before jelly beans) Jake

had always forgotten his uniform on game days. The AJB Jake had coded an app to remind him of what to bring to school each day.

And now he really looked forward to game days.

Thanks to some random combination of IK chewables, Jake was suddenly a whiz at basketball. A true all-star.

Kojo was also on the team. And he was an excellent player. Just not Jake McQuade excellent.

"You ready to tell me how you sink those three-pointers?" Kojo asked as the two friends put on their uniforms in the locker room after school.

Since the jelly beans, Jake had become something of a legend in the middle school league. People posted videos of him on YouTube. He never dribbled beyond the three-point line. He'd just plant himself on the far side of the zone, wait for one of his friends to pass him the ball, put up a perfectly angled shot, and watch it drop through the hoop.

"It's pretty complicated physics," Jake explained.

"Oh. I get it. You don't want to share your secret with me because you want to be the only superstar on this team. That's greedy, bro. You need to share the love."

"Okay, fine." Jake finished tying his laces. "You need to focus on three things to make every three-point shot."

Kojo leaned in. "Shhhh. Not so loud. We don't want everybody else to know our secret."

Jake launched into a whispered and detailed description of angle, velocity, wind resistance, and backspin.

Kojo held up his hand, his eyes pleading for Jake to stop.

"Wait," said Jake. "I haven't even mentioned trajectory speed."

"That's okay. I'll just wait for Mr. Farooqi to make me one of those basketball-physics jelly beans. Come on. Let's go show these dudes from Chumley Prep how we play ball at Riverview."

Kojo, Jake, and the rest of the Riverview Pirates hit the court. Chumley Prep, that afternoon's opponent, didn't stand a chance.

Kojo, Hargun Singh, Luke Rawcliffe, and Giacomo Saracino fed Jake the ball and encouraged him with their patter.

"Make it rain, baby!" shouted Kojo.

"McQuade is McAutomatic!" added Giacomo.

"Jakin' it from downtown!" cheered Luke, with a "Boo-yah" from Hargun.

Jake would plant himself beyond the three-point line and toss up perfectly angled shots with the appropriate backspin and velocity to swish through the hoop with nothing but net.

Every time.

SWISH!

He never missed.

SWISH!

With a few on-the-fly recalculations, he could even nail the net from half-court.

SWISH!

At the end of the first half, he arced a buzzer-beater all the way up court from underneath the opponent's basket.

SWOOSH!

Yes. He was showing off.

The final score was Riverview 99, Chumley Prep 12.

Jake was the basketball team's star. He was the school's most brilliant scholar. He had major corporations and government officials calling him for advice.

And he loved every minute of it.

He just didn't know how much longer any of it might last.

6

Zane Zinkle sat snuggled in the upholstered cocoon of his white egg chair in his sterile white office.

His fingers formed a pup tent under his nose. He was thinking. Using his gigantic brain.

It's what he did best.

It's what he'd always done.

When he was six months old, he told his pediatrician, "I think I have an infection in my left ear." And he did.

Zinkle learned to read when he was ten months old. He graduated from high school at the age of six. College when he was ten. He was even in the *Guinness World Records* book as "the world's smartest child."

Until Jake McQuade came along. Jake. The young freckle-faced fool had usurped Zinkle's historic ranking.

The boy needed to be dealt with.

Immediately.

Zinkle's enormous corporate headquarters stood behind high security fencing and a moat in the secluded, forested suburbs north of the city. Zinkle Inc. was the second-most profitable company in the world.

Second.

Zane Zinkle hated that word. That's why he had bold and secret plans to catapult his company up to the top slot.

Soon. Very soon.

His dome-shaped office atop Zinkle Inc.'s massive four-story, tinted-glass building looked like the bridge on the starship *Enterprise*.

Because Zinkle was a Trekkie.

He'd also masterminded the first quantum computers and reinvented the smartphone. His coveted zPhone was three times as good and three times more expensive than any other device on the market.

Zinkle controlled acres of cloud server farms on his sprawling campus. And thanks to his artificially intelligent Virtuoso supercomputer, Zinkle knew everything there was to know about anything.

Except the answer to one nagging question: *How did Jake McQuade get so smart so quickly?*

Zinkle knew the twelve-year-old slacker's history. Until a few months ago, Jake Quincy McQuade was the laziest, least motivated student at Riverview Middle School. He was a C student. He was terrible at basketball. He spoke no foreign languages.

Then, all of a sudden, he became a certified genius with "an IQ well in excess of three hundred."

Zinkle's own IQ had tested at 290.

The professors who administered the IQ test declared that Jake McQuade "is, without a doubt, the smartest kid in the universe."

That used to be Zinkle's claim to fame.

Now Zane Zinkle had to crush Jake McQuade. To erase him from the record books.

Zinkle had only sponsored the e-games tournament at the Imperial Marquis Hotel because he knew the boy's mother was the events coordinator there. She would tell Jake. Jake would want to play. Once a gamer, always a gamer. Mrs. McQuade had served her purpose. She'd helped lure her genius son closer to Zinkle's web.

"McQuade defeated Virtuoso," Zinkle seethed as he swiveled slightly in his egg-shaped chair. He stared at the eight-inch-tall soft rubber modern-art sculpture of a polar bear in the center of his desk. It was the voice-activated data portal into Virtuoso.

"Hey, Lulu?" Zinkle said to the bear.

"Yes, Mr. Zinkle?"

"Play me the trout stream. The babbling brook."

The soothing sounds of water trickling across smooth stones took Zinkle back to the one happy day he remembered from his childhood. Fishing. With his father. The trout stream sounds Lulu generated helped Zinkle think more clearly.

"No one defeats my quantum computer," he muttered to himself and the imaginary trout. "It makes me look weak. Worse. It makes me seem . . ." He could barely say the ugliest word ever uttered. "Ignorant!"

Suddenly, inspiration struck—just as it always did when you're smarter than everybody in the room.

Zinkle tapped the head of the bear to cut off the soundscape.

He had a plan. An evil, nefarious, diabolical plan.

Jake McQuade would prove no match for Zane Zinkle.

"I can outsmart him," Zinkle told himself. "I can outsmart anyone. I am, and always will be, the smartest person in the universe. It's time to launch Operation Brain Drain!"

7

"What's for dinner tonight?" Jake's mother asked him.

"I was thinking Caribbean jerk shrimp with avocado cream sauce over pineapple and tomato rice," he said, stifling a yawn. Whipping up gourmet food for his family—based on *MasterChef Junior* recipes he just seemed to know—had become so easy it was actually kind of boring.

"Sounds great," said his mom, glancing at the clock on the microwave. It was nearly seven.

"But hurry," added Emma. "I'm starving."

"Or," said Jake, "we could simply enjoy a yeasted flatbread topped with tomato sauce and cheese that someone else bakes in an oven, preheated to five hundred and fifty degrees."

"You mean pizza?" said his mom.

"Yeah. Pizza."

After their pizza dinner, Emma needed help with her math homework.

Jake took the paper and, while munching on a stack of Oreos with one hand, quickly filled in all the answer blanks with his free hand.

"I thought you could help me learn how to do the math by myself," said Emma, pouting her lips.

"Nah," said Jake, a shower of cookie crumbs spewing out of his mouth. "This way's faster. Easier, too."

"Thanks," muttered Emma. She shuffled out of Jake's room, shaking her head and rolling her eyes. Sometimes her brainy big brother could be sooooo disappointing.

The next day at school, during fifth period, Jake went to the new special he'd been doing for a few weeks: tech ed.

Mr. Green was the teacher and had eagerly adopted Grace, Kojo, and Jake's cool idea for a "recycling machine" as the class's term project. Grace had come up with a way to help deal with what she called "the swarm of plastic bottles threatening our oceans." Kojo had designed the contraption. Jake had tackled some of the thornier engineering issues and shared all sorts of ecology facts (like the stats on the Great Pacific Garbage Patch, which was twice the size of Texas). The kids in Mr. Green's tech ed class were actually constructing it.

Luke Rawcliffe, from the basketball team, was the star of tech ed. There was nothing the guy couldn't build. On the other hand, Jake was kind of a klutz when it came to tool-based knowledge—even after eating all those jelly beans.

"We need to tighten these screws," said Luke, pressing the corner of the sheet metal panel on the gizmo's side. "They're a little loose."

Jake handed him a hammer.

Luke looked around to make sure nobody was listening. "Um, you don't hammer screws, Jake," he whispered. "Grab me a hex-head screwdriver."

"Gotcha," said Jake. He rummaged through the toolbox and handed Luke a screwdriver.

"That's a Phillips head," said Luke softly. He was one of the nicest people at Riverview, which was why he was trying his best not to embarrass Jake. That was a good thing. Because Jake was already doing an excellent job embarrassing himself.

"A hex head has six sides," Luke explained.

"Like a hexagon!" said Jake, happy to be back in the familiar jelly bean territory of geometry.

Luke shrugged. "I guess."

Jake finally found the correct tool and handed it to Luke.

"Thanks, man," said Luke.

Jake just nodded. And wondered what other gaping holes still remained in his knowledge base.

Would those holes expand, widen, and grow like Swiss cheese melting in a microwave? What if everything he'd learned so quickly vanished the same way—quickly?

It was possible. Because even Haazim Farooqi wasn't sure how long the "meritorious effects" of his IK capsules would "remain stable."

"Nothing lasts forever, my young friend," Farooqi had once told Jake. "In fact, scientifically speaking, it is quite likely that forever does not even exist. This is why we can no longer enjoy new episodes of *The Office* or *Friends*. It's also why bubble gum loses its flavor."

There was a rap of knuckles on the classroom's open door. Principal Lyons stuck in his head. Kojo was with him.

"Excuse me, Mr. Green," Mr. Lyons said to the tech ed teacher. "We need to borrow Jake for a very important . . . *conversation*."

8

Jake and Kojo followed Mr. Lyons up the hall to the principal's office.

Everything in the school was sparkling clean and brand-new. The lockers. The linoleum floor tiles. Even the drinking fountains were the kind that could refill your bottle with filtered water.

"As you know, guys," said Mr. Lyons as they walked, "thanks to your generous contributions, we have made quite a few improvements to this school building and campus."

"You made a jumbo-sized donation, too," Jake reminded Mr. Lyons.

"True," Mr. Lyons said with a proud smile. "As did, of course, Grace."

"She's the richest kid in the world," said Kojo. "But she doesn't have a mansion or a limo."

"She has a closet full of sneakers," said Mr. Lyons.

"True. But she needs a mansion and a limo. I know I'd have one. Maybe two. If I had her money, I'd live in two mansions and take a limo back and forth between 'em. 'Oh, my hat's in my other house'? Limo ride. 'Forgot my basketball in my other garage'? Limo ride!"

"That not how Grace rolls," said Jake.

"Thank goodness," added Mr. Lyons. "But we've just been presented with an opportunity to do even more for Riverview Middle School. It could really be a big bonus for our faculty, staff, and students."

"Somebody wants to sponsor a YouTube channel of Jake dropping all those three-pointers from half-court?" said Kojo.

Mr. Lyons laughed. "No. Not yet, anyhow. Come into my office, guys. Zane Zinkle wants to FaceChat with us."

"The Zanester?" said Kojo as if it were no big deal. He took in a deep, chest-filling breath. "Yeah, we met ZZ at the e-games tournament. He probably still wants that selfie with Jake. I don't know why he didn't just call me. I gave him a business card. Gave his assistant one, too."

"He has a very interesting proposition to make," said Mr. Lyons. "A partnership. Between Zinkle Inc., Jake, and this school."

"What sort of partnership?" asked Jake.

They reached the main office. Mr. Lyons held open the door and indicated that Jake and Kojo should head on in.

"I'll let Mr. Zinkle explain it to you."

"Fine," said Kojo, striding past the reception desk and into Mr. Lyons's corner office. "But, Jake?"

"Yeah?"

"Don't agree to anything until I give you the signal."

Kojo touched the side of his nose.

"Is that the signal?"

"Nah. My nose is just itchy."

9

Mr. Lyons gestured for Jake to sit down in the swivel chair directly in front of the desktop computer.

He mouse-clicked the FaceChat icon, and the screen dissolved into a close-up of a very serious-looking young woman in a black turtleneck sweater and round, invisible-frame glasses.

"Please stand by for Mr. Zinkle."

"Standing by!" hollered Kojo from off camera.

That startled the lady. She clicked her keyboard and was replaced by Zane Zinkle.

"Hello, Jake. Congratulations again on defeating my smartest, most technologically advanced computer."

"Thank you, Mr. Zinkle."

"Jake," Zinkle continued, his smile widening, "you are a genius. A certifiable genius. I've heard your IQ is over two hundred and ninety."

"Three hundred," said Kojo from off screen.

Zinkle smiled. Nodded. Blinked. His face looked like it hurt again. Eventually, he continued.

"Brains like yours—and, of course, mine—are what power Zinkle Inc., Jake. For Zinkle to grow into the future, to become the world's most profitable company, we need the best and brightest thinkers of your generation to join us as we march forward toward an even smarter, more intelligent, more lucrative tomorrow."

Kojo stuck his head into the camera's frame.

"Excuse me. Kojo Shelton. Jake's manager. But you knew that. You have one of my cards. By the way, those things cost like five cents each. I could get them cheaper, but then I'd have to print a ton and, between you and me, I don't want to carry that much cardboard around, know what I mean?"

"Yes. I suppose I do."

"Cool. Okay. Here's my question. Are you making Jake a job offer? Do you want him to quit school and come work for you at Zinkle Inc., which, if you ask me, you should rebrand as Zinkle Inkle. It's catchier. Has pizzazz. 'Zinkle Inkle.' Can you feel that poetry? That's free marketing advice, Mr. Z. No charge."

Somehow, Zinkle's grin grew even wider. He looked like the wolf from "Little Red Riding Hood."

"No, Mr. Shelton. I'm not offering Jake a job. Not today. I am simply FaceChatting with you folks to invite Mr. McQuade and, of course, his extremely savvy marketing manager to join the best and brightest young prodigies from all across the land at my first-ever Genius Camp, to be held here on the sprawling Zinkle campus starting next week. If you two attend, I will adopt Riverview Middle School."

"We have to come live with you?" said Kojo. "All of us?"

"Hardly. But when I adopt your school, every single student, teacher, and staff member will receive a brand-new, fully loaded Zinkle Eleven smartphone."

Jake's jaw dropped. "The zPhone Eleven? The one that's three times more expensive than any other smartphone?"

Zinkle nodded. "It only costs that much because it's three times smarter. Just like me. So, what do you say, Jake? Do we have a deal?"

10

Just then, Jake's ordinary non-zPhone started buzzing in his pocket.

"Excuse me, sir," he said to Mr. Zinkle. "I need to look at this. It could be something urgent."

"Of course," said Zinkle. "Of course."

Jake glanced down at his device.

> RU available? If so, Special Agent Andrus will meet you outside the school. Immediately.

It was a text from Deputy Assistant Director Don Struchen of the FBI. Not too long ago, Jake had used his smarts to help Struchen solve a complicated and perplexing problem. Now it looked like he had another one. Special Agent Patrick Andrus had been involved with that first case, too.

"Jake?" asked Principal Lyons. "Is everything okay?"

"Not sure." Jake looked back at Zane Zinkle's image on the screen. "Mr. Zinkle? It *is* something urgent. The FBI might need me to work another case with them."

Zinkle's left eye twitched slightly. "I see. The FBI? Well, well, well . . ."

Kojo stepped into the computer camera's field of vision.

"But we love your offer," he said. "I've had my eye on a zPhone since forever. So I'm sure Jake will—"

"Seriously consider your Genius Camp idea," said Jake before Kojo could finish. "But first I need to help the FBI."

"No, you don't," whispered Kojo. "You can multi-task, baby."

"Kojo's right," added the principal. "You're very good at juggling three things at once."

It was true. Literally. The knowledge required to toss and catch a number of objects so as to keep at least one in the air while handling the others had been in one of Farooqi's jelly beans.

But Jake wasn't sure he wanted to go to a camp filled with genius kids from all over the country. Plus, the last time Jake went to camp, he got a rash. He also wasn't thrilled with the whole "latrine" situation.

Besides, like Mr. Farooqi said, nothing lasts forever! What if the jelly beans suddenly wore off?

What if his three-hundred-plus IQ disappeared overnight?

What if none of the other geniuses wanted to see him do dumb stuff like juggle fruit?

Deep down, Jake still doubted his new superpowers. Deep down, he still felt like a phony.

"When does your Genius Camp start?" Jake asked Zinkle.

"This coming Monday. It will only require a one-week commitment."

"You guys can miss classes for a week," said Mr. Lyons. "We'll call it an independent-study field trip. After all, you're both A-plus students."

"True," said Kojo. "And I've been pulling down those A-pluses my whole school career. Unlike some—"

Jake cut Kojo off again. "Let me think about it, okay, Mr. Zinkle? Let me see if I can wrap up this FBI thing first."

"Of course," said Zinkle. "Of course. Go solve your crime with the FBI. That sounds like oodles of fun. Of course, they've never asked me for any assistance. . . ." He sighed. And, for just a second, he looked like a pouty puppy. But then he flashed that toothy smile back across his face. "I just need to know by Sunday. Nine a.m. At the latest. I want to make sure we order enough marshmallows."

"Marshmallows?" said Jake.

"It's camp," explained Kojo. "We're going to be making s'mores. You can't call yourself a camper if you're not making s'mores, am I right, Mr. Z?"

"Precisely," said Mr. Zinkle.

"We'll get back to you by nine Sunday morning," said Jake. "I promise."

"You want to give me your home number, Mr. Z?" said Kojo.

"No need," said Zinkle. "When you reach your decision, Jake, drop me a text."

Jake's phone dinged and thrummed.

He looked down at the screen. It was a smiley face from Zane Zinkle.

"How'd you know my cell number?" Jake wondered aloud.

Zinkle's smile stretched a little wider and a little tighter. It looked like it might snap. "It's what I do, Jake. I know things. I look forward to your response and hope it will be in the affirmative. We're searching for this company's leaders of tomorrow today!"

"But we have until Sunday," said Kojo. "Today's only Thursday. So you can't, you know, find your leaders of tomorrow *today*—unless you change the deadline."

Zinkle blinked. Repeatedly. "Correct."

"Talk to you on Sunday, baby," said Kojo. "Over and out."

11

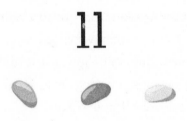

"So? Are you going to camp?" asked Grace, who'd just stepped into the principal's office.

"They're thinking about it," said Mr. Lyons. "Right, Jake?"

"Yeah. I'm thinking."

"Stand back, everybody," joked Kojo. "When Jake McQuade starts thinking, steam shoots out of his ears."

Grace laughed. "It's only a week, Jake. And it's camp. Camp is fun. Especially if Kojo is going with you."

Kojo nodded. "It's true. They do call me Mr. Fun. You should come, too, Grace."

"No can do. I need to stay here and work on the mayor. We're *this* close to landing a meeting with her and doing our bit to save the planet."

Jake tried to protest. "But—"

"Just think about all the good you two could do," said

Grace. "All those free phones loaded with apps? A lot of kids at this school could never afford a zPhone."

"Couldn't you just buy everybody one?" Jake asked.

"Sure. I guess. But, somehow, I just think it's going to mean a whole lot more coming from you. You'd be sharing your gifts with the whole school."

"Plus," said Kojo, "the zPhones would be free."

Grace grinned. "Yeah. There's that. . . ."

Jake still wasn't sure.

"I, uh, need to go see what this is all about," he said, wiggle-waggling his phone.

"FBI," Kojo told Grace, taking in a deep, chest-billowing breath. "They need us. Again. Come on, Jake. Can't keep the feds waiting. You do, they'll audit your taxes."

"Jake doesn't pay taxes," said Grace.

"But one day he will," said Kojo. "Come on."

Kojo and Jake strode out of the principal's office.

"What's our situation?" asked Kojo.

Jake shrugged. "Not sure."

"What's their twenty?"

"Huh?"

"Their ten-twenty. That's the classic FBI radio code for 'location.' You have a dog case? That's a ten-eleven. Ten-ninety-four? Drag racing. Come on, man. Work with me."

"The text just said Agent Andrus would meet me out front."

"You want me to roll with you and Andrus?"

Jake shook his head. "No. I think I'll just fly solo."

Kojo stopped in his tracks. "Seriously? Even though you don't know any of the FBI's 'ten' codes? You think you can do this on your own? Without me?"

"Ten-four," said Jake. "That means 'yes.'"

"I know what ten-four means, man. Everybody knows that one. But I'm the dude who told you what all those other tens mean!"

"Look—I need to see if I can do this on my own."

"Huh?"

Jake checked to make sure nobody was listening. Especially Grace. Fortunately, she and Mr. Lyons were still in the office. Jake wasn't great with the whole "discussing his feelings" thing. But his life had been such a whirlwind since he ate the jelly beans, he had to tell someone. Kojo had been his best friend since second grade. If Jake was going to tell anybody, it'd be Kojo.

"I'm afraid," Jake admitted.

"Afraid? Of what?"

"Losing it."

"Losing what?"

"My smarts! Everyone expects me to be all brilliant all the time. What if it disappears? Mr. Farooqi still hasn't replicated his original jelly beans, and we don't know if or when the IK capsules I ate will wear off and stop working."

"Oh man, are you still worried about that?"

"Constantly." It felt so good to finally say it out loud.

"Relax," said Kojo. "It's baked into your cake. You're not going to 'lose it.' You are a permanent genius."

"How can you be so sure?"

"Did Spider-Man ever lose his Spidey powers?"

"No."

"And he only got bit by *one* radioactive spider. You ate a whole jar of jelly beans. You know everything."

"Only because I cheated and took a shortcut. I didn't study or read a ton of textbooks. Even Mr. Farooqi isn't one hundred percent certain how it all works or how long it lasts."

"Oh. I get it. This is why you didn't want to say yes to Zane Zinkle. You're afraid all those other brainiacs at Genius Camp might be mean to you if you're not as smart as they are. Well, let me give it to you straight, Jake McQuade: you are smarter than absolutely everybody on earth, Zane Zinkle included."

"I'm not so sure. That's why I want to do this FBI thing, whatever it is, on my own. I need to prove that I'm still supersmart."

"What? Who do you need to prove that to?"

"Me, Kojo. *Me.*"

Kojo sighed. "Okay, okay. I get it. When you're ten-twenty-four on the case, you'll feel better."

"Huh?"

"Ten-twenty-four. Assignment completed."

"Exactly. And, Kojo?"

"Yeah?"

"Thanks for understanding."

"I'm cool. We're cool. But the next FBI gig?"

Jake nodded. "You're definitely coming with me."

12

Kojo pushed the exit bar on the front door and held it open for Jake.

A sleek black sedan with government plates was parked in the drop-off lane.

"Go on," said Kojo. "Don't make Special Agent Andrus wait. If he gets stuck behind the school buses, you two aren't ever making it down to DC."

"Thanks, Kojo."

Jake hurried out to the waiting car and climbed into the back seat.

"Good to see you again, Mr. McQuade," said Special Agent Andrus from behind the wheel. A special agent Jake hadn't met before was sitting up front in the passenger seat. She had blond hair tied back in a ponytail. Both agents wore dark suits, even darker sunglasses, and Secret Service–style earpieces.

"This is Special Agent Kellie Otis," said Andrus.

"Pleasure to meet you, Mr. McQuade," said Otis. She was as brusque and to the point as Andrus.

"Nice to meet you, too. Is it, uh, okay if I call my mom?"

"Make it quick," said Otis. "Deputy Assistant Director Struchen is waiting for us. We needed to be on the jet five minutes ago."

"We're taking a jet?"

"Gulfstream 550. It's waiting for us on the tarmac."

Jake worked his phone. Andrus placed a swirling blue light on the dashboard and sped away from the school.

"Hi, Mom," Jake said into the phone. "Yeah. I won't be home for dinner. I might need to spend the night down in DC, too."

"We're not going to DC." Agent Otis tossed the remark over her shoulder.

"Um, Mom? We're going someplace. Not sure where. It's a new FBI thing. Yes, Mom. I'll make sure to eat something on the plane. Oh, is it okay if I miss my turn taking out the garbage next week? I might be going to camp. Genius Camp."

Jake climbed into the sleek Gulfstream 550 jet with Special Agents Andrus and Otis.

"So, uh, where are we going?" Jake asked after buckling himself into one of the private jet's very comfy seats. It was a classier version of his grandpa's recliner.

There were free sodas, plastic-wrapped sandwiches,

and chip bags waiting in the galley. Jake couldn't eat anything until the plane reached a comfortable cruising altitude. Jake had learned that when he popped open a bag of Cool Ranch Doritos before finding his seat. Agent Andrus had taken the Doritos away.

"We're heading to Arizona," said Agent Otis as the jet smoothly lifted off. "A deserted spot just outside Phoenix. Deputy Assistant Director Struchen will meet us there."

"What's our situation?" said Jake, trying his best to sound like Kojo because Kojo always sounded cool and confident, no matter the situation.

"Something that should be of particular interest to you," said Agent Andrus. "Buried treasure."

When the plane reached cruising altitude, Jake and the two agents sat around a worktable covered with a map and crime scene photos.

Andrus and Otis took Jake through the case file.

Turns out, the FBI suspected that a notorious inter-national jewel thief they'd been trailing for years, named Desmond "Sir Slip 'N Slide" Higginbottom, had stolen diamonds worth five million dollars from a high-end jewelry store in Beverly Hills—across the Arizona border in California.

"But," admitted Andrus, "we can't connect him to the crime. We *think* he buried his treasure near a paloverde tree in a secluded spot not far from Phoenix."

Otis picked up the tale. "We call Higginbottom 'Sir Slip 'N Slide' because he has a phony British accent and, so far, we've never been able to gather enough evidence to arrest him. He slips out of our grip and slides on to his next heist."

"We don't want to lose him again," said Andrus. "That's why we need you and your brain."

Jake swallowed hard. The pressure was on. What if he needed some kind of tool to crack the case? How could Luke Rawcliffe show him which one to use? Luke wasn't on the plane!

The FBI assumed Higginbottom had buried the storage container full of stolen diamonds, intending to come back and retrieve it after the "heat died down."

"But," said Agent Otis, "he was lazy."

Jake could relate. Jake used to be so lazy that instead of pushing a button on the remote, he'd actually wait fifteen seconds for the next episode of a show he was streaming to start.

"He didn't bury his box very deep. Maybe only a foot. There was a downpour, followed by a flash flood. The sandy soil washed away. The bin was exposed in its shallow pit."

"Soon afterward," Andrus continued, "an extremely honest motorcyclist saw something gleaming in the sun as he cruised up the highway. He went over, pried the lid off the container, took one look, and immediately recognized the merchandise as stolen goods. He called the local authorities. The locals noted that some of the items were still in boxes labeled 'Monsieur Francois's Fine Jewelry, Beverly Hills, California.' "

"That made it an interstate crime," said Otis. "The locals called us. We took over the case."

Unfortunately, as Special Agent Andrus explained, there was very little forensic evidence at the crime scene.

"Higginbottom knew to wear gloves so we couldn't lift any fingerprints. He probably wore a hairnet and other protective gear, because we didn't find any hair or trace particles. He even knew to wash down everything with bleach to eliminate any trace of DNA evidence he might've left behind."

"However," said Otis, "we did find something very interesting when we impounded his pickup truck."

"What?" asked Jake.

"Two bean pods in the bed," said Andrus. "Bean pods from a paloverde tree."

"That's good," said Jake. "But it's not good enough. Sure, it might mean that Higginbottom parked his truck near the paloverde tree at the treasure site. Or it just might be a random coincidence because, unfortunately, the paloverde tree grows everywhere in Arizona. In fact, on April ninth, 1954, the governor signed legislation that declared the paloverde the official tree of Arizona."

Andrus turned to Otis and grinned. "See? I told you. This kid knows everything about anything."

"Well, let's just hope he knows how to link Higginbottom to *our* paloverde tree."

"I might," said Jake. "I might."

His brain started whirring, making connections. It was his favorite part of being smart. It made him feel the same way he did working a jigsaw puzzle.

"You still have the seed pods you found in the back of your suspect's truck, right?" he said.

"Of course," said Otis.

"Can your team collect more, random paloverde seed pods from different locations?"

"Uh, yeah," said Andrus. "Like you said: they're everywhere in Arizona."

"Excellent. Send them all to Dr. Noelle Griffith at Arizona State University in Tempe. I met her once at a seminar. My friend Grace's father, Professor Garcia, was the host. I went for the snacks. They had pigs in a blanket."

Agent Andrus nodded approvingly. "Those little hot dogs wrapped in flaky dough?"

"Where the dough soaks up the hot dog grease?" added Agent Otis. "Those are delish."

"Yeah. Anyway, Dr. Griffith is a brilliant plant geneticist. Have her run a randomly amplified polymorphic DNA test on the seed pods."

"A what?"

"An RAPD, or 'rapid' test. She'll understand."

"Oh-kay. And then what?"

"I'll need to investigate the crime scene."

"That's why Deputy Assistant Director Struchen is waiting for you there."

"Awesome. Oh—one more thing?"

"Yes?"

"Can I have those Doritos now?"

13

When the FBI jet landed in Phoenix, a hulking black SUV was waiting on the runway to greet it.

After exiting the airport, the SUV's tires were soon humming up a very long, very straight, and very empty stretch of highway lined with lots of low scrubby brush and drab dirt. The roadway shimmered in the heat, sending up a wavy mirage.

They passed a few paloverde trees showing off their brilliant yellow blossoms.

"Interestingly," said Jake, "the name *paloverde* is the Spanish word for 'green tree,' even though the trees are famous for their *yellow* flowers. The bark of the tree is green because it contains chlorophyll. The paloverde does its photosynthesizing through its bark, not its leaves like so many other trees."

All the FBI agents were staring at him. Even the driver. He was looking up at Jake in the rearview mirror.

About thirty minutes later, the vehicle crunched off the highway and pulled up to a taped-off CRIME SCENE DO NOT CROSS area.

Deputy Assistant Director Don Struchen was waiting on the far side of the barrier. He was with half a dozen field agents in navy-blue FBI windbreakers, many of them toting aluminum attaché cases and evidence-gathering equipment.

Struchen was a buttoned-up man, maybe in his fifties, with a snowy-white crew cut and a no-nonsense attitude about everything.

"Thanks for joining us on such short notice, Jake," he said. "Higginbottom's been a burr under my saddle for twenty years. So we need to move fast, while the evidence is still fresh."

"Happy to help, sir," said Jake. "If I can."

He didn't want to make any promises. He liked these guys and didn't want to disappoint them.

"At your suggestion," said Struchen, "our agents harvested seed pod samples all over the state. We've also contacted Dr. Griffith. She's running that DNA test you suggested."

"Cool," said Jake.

"Do you mind filling me in?" said Struchen. "What's cooking in that big brain of yours?"

Jake nodded toward the towering paloverde tree, with its shrubby canopy of yellowish-green leaves. "Is that our tree?"

"Ten-four," said Struchen. That made Jake smile. *Oh*

yeah. Next time, Kojo is definitely coming on any FBI field trips.

"Okay," said Jake. "You need to establish that the two bean pods you found in the bed of Higginbottom's pickup truck came from *this* paloverde tree and no other."

"Correct."

"So take a sample of the tree's bark and send it to Dr. Griffith. She'll try to match the two sets of plant DNA—one from the seed pods you found in the truck, one from the bark. That'll prove that your suspect was here at the scene of the crime. All those other seed pods your guys collected? That will show the jury that, just like humans, no two paloverde trees have identical DNA. That the seed pods could only have come from this one particular tree."

Struchen pursed his lips. Then he nodded.

"Zembruzski?" he shouted to a female tech wearing surgical gloves. "Scrape off a sample of that tree bark. Rush it to Dr. Griffith. Now!"

"Yes, sir!"

Struchen extended his hand and gave Jake a shake.

"You've still got it, Jake," he said proudly.

"Yes, sir. I think I do."

"We'll take it from here, son."

For whatever reason, Jake saluted.

"Andrus? Otis?" said Struchen. "Fly Mr. McQuade home. His job here is done."

"Great," said Jake, his confidence fully restored. "Because I have some packing to do. On Monday morning, I'm going to Genius Camp!"

14

Zane Zinkle paced in front of a whiteboard one of his flunkies, the one named Christina, had rolled into a spacious conference room at Zinkle World Headquarters.

There were six photographs, all of them headshots, evenly spaced across the board. They were held in place by crystal-clear magnets. Underneath each photo was a name and a brief biography.

Zinkle glared at the six photos on the board.

"These are the best and brightest children in all the land?" Zinkle said to Christina, once again adjusting his glasses with the tip of his pinky.

"Yes, sir," said Christina. She regularly bleached her long black hair to turn it white so it would match the interior decor of the Zinkle headquarters building. "One of these children could be the next you, sir."

Zinkle shot her a frosty look. "That can never happen, Christina. Never!"

"Of course not, sir. I was just making an unwanted and unnecessary observation. Sorry."

"It was a nasty observation, Christina. A horrible, rotten, terrible, stinky, no-good, poo-poo observation!" His face was nearly purple.

"I won't do it again, sir," said Christina. She had grown accustomed to her boss's childish tantrums. She'd had to. He paid her a lot of money.

Zinkle closed his eyes and took a deep cleansing breath.

"I'm fishing, I'm fishing, I'm fishing," he muttered to himself. He opened his eyes and turned to Christina. "Tell me about these six so-called geniuses."

"Of course, sir. First up is Jake McQuade. He has agreed to come to camp."

"Wonderful!" Zinkle rubbed his hands together gleefully. "Are we ready to adopt his school?"

"Yes, sir. Everything is in place. The zPhones will be delivered first thing Monday morning. McQuade will arrive at camp Monday afternoon."

"Excellent. Excellent. Riverview Middle School will be an ideal test market. The first step to making even more money." Zinkle closed his eyes, shook his fists as if they were pom-poms, and chanted, "We're number one! We're number one!"

Christina cleared her throat. "Now, then, sir, we have some background information on Jake—"

Zinkle's eyes popped open.

"I don't need or want to hear it! I know all about the smartest kid on the planet. That used to be me, Christina. Me!"

"I know, sir."

"My face was on the cover of magazines when I was nine years old."

"Yes, sir. I've seen them hanging in the hallways."

Zinkle clasped his hands behind his back and paced. Christina knew what was coming next. A monologue.

"I learned at a very early age that knowledge is power. The smartest person in any room can rule that room. The only threat to that power is if someone who thinks they're smarter comes along! If so, the reigning genius must use his superior smarts to crush his disrespectful opponent tout suite, which means immediately!"

"Yes, sir. We're on it, sir. Operation Brain Drain is ready to launch on your command."

"Good, good. Continue, Christina. Who is our next camper?"

"Mr. McQuade's best friend and business partner, Kojo Shelton."

Zinkle crinkled up his nose. "I received a paper cut from that business card he gave me. Young Mr. Shelton shall pay for that. Mark my words. He shall pay! I suspect he will also be the easiest to turn."

"That's not a given, sir. Don't let Mr. Shelton's 'cool dude' swagger and old-television-show obsession fool you. He is very, very intelligent. In fact, until a few months ago, he outscored every student at Riverview Middle School except a certain Grace Garcia."

"Oh, I've heard about Miss Garcia. They say she's the richest kid in the world."

"Yes, sir. Of course, she hasn't been extremely wealthy for very long. It's another sudden twist. Something to do with the discovery of her family's buried treasure."

"I hate her."

"Yes, sir. Understandable."

"I hate rich kids. Rich kids always had more toys than me. All I had was a bamboo fishing pole. That's why Grace Garcia is not invited to my camp! Not now. Not never!"

Christina ignored the petulant double negative and kept her gaze fixed on the board. She still had four campers left to go. She hoped she could make this quick.

"The others, all certified geniuses, are Abia Sulayman, Poindexter Perkins—"

"The boy's name is Poindexter? The name of the genius scientist in the *Felix the Cat* cartoons?"

"Yes, sir. His parents wanted their son to be a child prodigy like you. Some parents boost their baby's intelligence with Mozart music; some just name their son Poindexter. It worked."

"I hate him this much." Zinkle held his arms out wide as he sulked some more.

Christina powered on. "Next up is Dawn Yang from Palo Alto, California. At age fifteen, she already runs her own software development company."

"I hate her even more than Poindexter."

"Understood, sir. However, she might prove valuable. She is considered something of a tech wizard."

"Says who?"

"Various people."

"Well, I hate them, too. Who's this last brainiac?"

"Mackenzie Meekleman, sir."

"Does she own her own company?"

"No. She mumbles a lot."

"Hmmm? I didn't quite get that, Christina. You were mumbling!" He giggled.

Christina so hated her job.

But she so loved her six-figure salary.

"Very well," said Zinkle, glowering at the collection of young faces arrayed in front of him. "Camp starts Monday afternoon. You will be the head counselor. You will report to me on a daily basis. And, Christina?"

"Sir?"

"Do not let me down. You're a very bright and intelligent young woman. I wouldn't want anything to jeopardize your future here at Zinkle."

"Yes, sir."

Zinkle scuttled out the conference room door, chortling merrily.

"Ima gonna get you, Jake McQuade." His voice was singsongy. Like you'd hear on a playground. "Ima gonna get you!"

15

"I'm so proud of you, Jake," said Grace.

And then, *BOOM!* She surprised him with a cheek smack.

It was first thing Monday morning. Jake, Kojo, and Grace were standing near the front doors of Riverview Middle School, watching a crew of Zinkle Store employees—all of them in white pants and black polo shirts—roll in crates filled with shimmering shrink-wrapped zPhone boxes.

"We're going to distribute everything in the cafeteria at lunchtime, guys," said Mr. Lyons, coming out of his office with a woman with long white hair. Jake recognized her. She'd been one of Zane Zinkle's minions at the e-games tournament.

"Zinkle team members will help everybody set up their devices," said the lady, gesturing toward the army of young men and women, all of them with Zinkle Inc.'s tiny lightning bolt Z logo embroidered on their shirts. "We've included several free apps, including our extremely popular Tweedle."

"Tweedle?" said Kojo. "Never heard of it."

"It's new," said the woman, whose ID badge tagged her as Christina. "And don't worry, both you and Mr. McQuade will receive a fully loaded zPhone in your Genius Camp welcome packet later today. You will also be receiving other souvenirs, such as Genius Camp baseball caps, windbreakers, and sports bottles." Christina checked her zWatch. "Principal Lyons? We need to coordinate the livestream."

"Right. Guess what, guys. Mr. Zinkle himself is going to make a brief statement during this morning's announcements. Excuse me. I need to introduce Christina to the *Riverview News* crew."

Principal Lyons escorted the Zinkle exec up the corridor to the library.

When the Riverview Middle School building was completely renovated, a sophisticated video studio, complete with three cameras, a switcher, several computers, and a green screen, was set up in the library. The morning announcements were now made morning-newscast-style by a rotating group of student volunteers.

"Look how happy everybody is, Jake," said Grace. "You helped so many people by saying yes to Genius Camp."

"I still think you should come, too," Jake told her. "You've been smart way longer than me."

"It's true," said Kojo. "Remember how Jake used to be so lazy? And kind of a slob? You did *not* want to sit next to him on Taco Tuesday in the cafeteria, that's for sure. . . ."

Grace laughed. "You guys will have a blast. I'll keep working on the mayor. I was able to get through to her assistant by pretending to be a talent scout for *Quiz Zone*."

The bell rang.

"We'd better head to our homerooms," said Grace. "And, Jake?"

"Yeah?"

"Thanks again."

She leaned in to give him another quick kiss. This one hit the side of Jake's nose because she'd totally taken him by surprise and he flinched.

"Hey," said Kojo. "I'm going to nerd camp, too!"

Grace gave him a kiss on the cheek.

And then, as the two boys stood there in stunned silence, she turned and walked away.

"I think she uses strawberry lip gloss," said Jake dreamily.

"Is that what I'm smelling?" said Kojo. "I thought maybe you had strawberry jam on your toast this morning and missed your mouth."

The two friends headed up the hall to their homeroom with Mr. Keeney.

"So, you all packed for camp?" Jake asked.

"Oh yeah. My mom's dropping off my duffel bag right after school."

"Mine too."

"I hope you packed a lot of underwear and socks. We're going to be hanging with the Zinkle geeks for a whole week."

"Yeah," said Jake. "Let's hope the jelly beans last that long."

16

Jake and Kojo headed into Mr. Keeney's classroom.

Their homeroom teacher was wearing one of his math-inspired T-shirts. This one was an equation followed by some stacked words:

$$\sqrt{(-1)} \ 2^3 \ \Sigma \ \Pi$$

and it was

delicious.

"Ha!" said Jake. "Very funny."

"Thank you, Mr. McQuade," said Mr. Keeney, slurping coffee out of his Baby Yoda mug.

"What?" whispered Kojo. "What does it mean?"

"I ate some pie and it was delicious."

"Seriously?"

"Yeah."

"And you knew that?"

"Sure. The square root of negative one is 'i,' for 'imaginary number.' Two cubed is eight. The next symbol is for 'sum.' And the last symbol is 'pi.' I eight sum pi."

Kojo was nodding and grinning ear to ear. "Oh yeah. Those jelly beans are still bouncing around in your brain big-time, baby."

The morning news anchors read a few announcements, led everybody in the Pledge of Allegiance, and reminded folks that it was "Macaroni Monday" in the cafeteria.

"And today," said Xinyu Luo, the news anchor, "that mac and cheese will be served with a side order of zPhones, thanks to Jake McQuade, Kojo Shelton, and Riverview Middle School's new corporate sponsor, Zinkle Inc.!"

There was a prerecorded trumpet fanfare and Xinyu's face faded away as all the video monitors in the school shifted to the tech tycoon sitting at his white desk in front of a white wall. Zinkle, as always, was wearing a black turtleneck and pinky-sliding his glasses into place.

"Dude ought to invest in some anti-slip nose pads," grumbled Kojo.

Jake agreed. "Totally."

"Hello, boys and girls," said Zinkle sweetly, trying to sound like he was on *Sesame Street* or something. "I'm Zane Zinkle, chairman, CEO, and founder of Zinkle Inc."

"I still think they should call it Zinkle Inkle," muttered Kojo.

"It is my great honor to be adopting . . ."

Zinkle glanced down at a white lined note card on his desk.

"Riverview Middle School. Your classmates Jake McQuade and . . ."

He checked the card again.

"Cody Skeleton . . ."

Kojo rolled his eyes in disbelief. "Oh man."

". . . will be coming to my first-ever Genius Camp, where they will compete against four other brilliant young students arriving on the Zinkle campus from all across America."

"We're competing?" whispered Jake.

"It's camp," said Kojo. "You know. Tug-of-war. Horseshoes. Potato sack races. Camps always have games. Competitions."

"These will be no ordinary camp games or competitions," said Zinkle on the screen.

"Okay," said Kojo. "Scratch the potato sack races."

"These will be challenging mind games. Baffling brain benders. Mental gymnastics of the highest order."

"I'd rather play tug-of-war," muttered Jake.

"The camper who emerges as the smartest genius of them all after one week of intensive challenges will, after graduating from college—which, by the way, I did when I was ten years old—have a job waiting here at Zinkle Inc., where smarter is better, but smartest is best!"

17

That afternoon, the school threw Jake and Kojo a "Happy Camper" bon voyage party in the lobby.

There was sherbet punch, cake, cookies, and, of course, balloons. Jake and Kojo were wearing their very cool Z-slash Genius Camp baseball caps.

"We're so proud of you, Jake!" gushed his mother, who'd left work early to attend the big send-off. She'd also brought Jake his duffel bag loaded with clothes and stuff he might need over the next week. Like deodorant. Jake needed a lot of deodorant.

"My friends at school made you a card, Jake," said Emma. She handed him a big sheet of green construction paper folded in half. *Diviértete en el campamento nerdo* was written across the front in purple glitter. The greeting was in Spanish because Emma went to a Spanish-immersion school.

Jake smiled. Thinking about how he had learned Spanish without the help of the jelly beans made him realize that his superpower was one he could've given himself. He might've been able to become supersmart just by studying super hard. Maybe he could do the same thing at Genius Camp if the going got tough.

"'Have fun at nerd camp,'" he said, translating Emma's card out loud. "Thanks, sis." He gave her a hug. "I'll hang this over my bunk."

Kojo's mother had also come to the party with his duffel. His father was stuck at the office.

Kojo handed his mom a brand-new zPhone in its shiny black box and she started laughing. Hard. Mrs. Shelton had the jolliest laugh Jake had ever heard.

"I'll miss you, kiddo," she said, smothering Kojo in a huge hug. "But maybe this zPhone will help me pass the time." She laughed some more. "See you in a week, honey."

Jake showed a shiny zPhone box to his mother and sister. "Every student got one of these today at lunch. But Kojo and I will also get one up at Genius Camp. So this is for you, Emma."

"Woo-hoo!" said his sister.

Jake's mother intercepted the pass-off.

"No devices until fifth grade."

Emma was in fourth.

"Aw, Mom."

"Sorry. Rules are rules. We'll keep this someplace safe."

70

Emma elevated an eyebrow. "Like inside your purse?"

"Good idea. Thanks for the suggestion!"

And Mrs. McQuade tucked the brand-new zPhone 11 into her shoulder bag.

18

About four o'clock, a limo bus pulled up in the drop-off lane in front of the school.

There was a silver *Z* painted on the side. All of its windows were tinted smoky gray.

"Well, that's our ride," announced Jake.

"The Z-mobile!" added Kojo.

"Have fun, you guys!" said Grace, giving both of her friends one last hug. There were no kisses this time. That was a good thing. The school lobby was crowded. People were watching.

Jake and Kojo said one last goodbye to their mothers, grabbed their duffels, waved their hats to the cheering crowd, and headed off to board the Genius Camp bus.

They had the whole back of the spacious vehicle to themselves.

"Guess everybody else is flying in on private jets and

helicopters," mused Kojo. "Wish we lived farther away. Jets and helicopters are even cooler than a limo bus."

"We should call Mr. Farooqi," Jake suggested. "Let him know where we'll be for the next week."

"Good idea," said Kojo. "But hang on."

He scooted up to the front of the plush seating area to check out the privacy window separating the passengers from the driver. Kojo cupped his hands over his mouth and declared, very loudly, "Whoo! I just pooped my pants! It's bad, man. Made a big ol' mess back here."

The limo bus's tires kept humming along. The driver, reflected in the rearview mirror, remained stone-faced. The privacy window did not slide down.

"Okay. You're cool to make the call. That divider is soundproof, baby."

"Or the driver is a very good actor," said Jake.

"True. Could be one of those corporate spies I've seen in movies. So keep your call off speakerphone. Use your earbuds. You can fill me in later."

Jake pressed Farooqi's speed dial number on his current phone. He really wasn't looking forward to loading all his old data into the new zPhone waiting for him at Genius Camp. In fact, he probably wouldn't. Too much work. His old phone was fine. Hey, being supersmart hadn't cured *all* his laziness.

Farooqi answered on the first ring.

"Subject One? Is everything okay?"

"Yeah. We're fine. Just wanted to let you know that

Kojo and I are going to be spending the next week up at the Zinkle campus in Northchester County."

"Ah! Zinkle Incorporated! The brainchild of Zane Zinkle, who, once upon a time, was the smartest kid in the universe. But then you and I came along and took away his crown. It gives me great joy to think of such things."

Jake chuckled. "Anyway, if, you know, you have any breakthroughs . . ."

"Oh, I am getting close, Subject One. Very, very close. In fact, I am, at this very moment, pouring what I hope will be a booster bean into its mold."

"A booster bean? What subject?"

"Well, you're already a gourmet chef, so I thought I'd give you an upgrade in the culinary arts."

Jake heard smacking noises.

"Um, Mr. Farooqi? What's going on?"

"Sorry. Missed the mold. Dribbled a little of the syrup on my fingers. *Mmm.* Crushed Pineapple. Tangy."

"Shouldn't you be wearing sterile gloves?"

"Yes. I should. But, unfortunately, I am not."

Now Jake heard wet licking.

"Mr. Farooqi?"

"Sorry. But this Crushed Pineapple flavor is quite scrumptious. Oh, by the way, Subject One, did you know that a chef's hat, officially called a toque, is traditionally made with one hundred pleats to represent the one hundred different ways to cook an egg? Also, the black sapote is a fruit that tastes like chocolate pudding. It's native to Central and South America. Béchamel sauce, one of the most basic sauces in French cuisine, is made from a white roux and milk. White roux, of course, being a mixture of butter and flour."

Jake's eyes went wide.

"Mr. Farooqi?"

"Yes, Subject One?"

"How do you know all that culinary stuff?"

There was a pause. "I don't know."

"I do! You licked your fingers!"

"True. But I also do that whenever I eat Kentucky Fried Chicken."

"You sampled the new jelly bean, sir. The culinary booster. It worked. You've reconstituted your original recipe!"

"I did? I mean, yes, I did!"

"Did you write down the formula?"

Another pause.

"Let me get back to you on that."

Jake had to laugh. "Mr. Farooqi? You're the real genius!"

"Perhaps. But I don't have time to join you at Mr. Zinkle's camp. I have a recipe to write down, and it isn't for fancy French butter sauce!"

19

The Zinkle campus—or the Zinkleplex, as it was known in the tech world—was spread across fifty-two forested acres twenty miles north of the city.

The limo bus passed through a tall wall of hedges (hiding chain-link fencing topped with coiled barbed wire) and stopped at a security gate on a narrow bridge.

To get to the headquarters building, which loomed on the horizon like a four-story-tall aluminum-and-glass box, vehicles had to first convince the security folks in the gatehouse that they belonged there and then drive across a bridge over a moat.

"Check it out," said Kojo, admiring the building. "That domed flying-saucer thing up top must be Zane Zinkle's penthouse office."

"Or it could be the command deck from the starship *Enterprise.*"

"Because," said Kojo, "Zinkle is a Trekkie. I did my homework, baby."

The setting sun was reflected off the glass walls of the sprawling headquarters building.

"They say this is a great place to work," said Jake, picturing what his grown-up life might look like. "You get all sorts of perks. There's a barbershop, swim-in-place swimming pools, Ping-Pong and foosball tables, nap pods, a dry cleaner, scooters for traveling from one side of the building to the other, Lego tables. Plus free meals, snacks, and beverages, all day, every day."

Kojo tossed up his hands. "Why would anybody want to leave?"

"They don't!"

The limo bus crossed the narrow bridge and made a right turn onto what felt like a winding country road under a canopy of leafy trees. There was other traffic. Electric scooters. Golf carts. Those one-wheel motorized skateboard deals. Zinkle employees were bustling from building to building. Some structures were marked with signs identifying their purpose. Some weren't. The ones without any markers also didn't have any windows.

"That's where they do the *top*-top-secret stuff," said Kojo. "The unmarked buildings."

Jake nodded. "I bet you're right."

The limo bus wound its way through the woods until it came to a cul-de-sac wrapped around a manicured circle of grass. A flagpole was planted in its center. A Z! flag snapped in the breeze.

Several high-tech tiny houses elevated on angled metal struts were arrayed around the rim of the circular roadway. They looked like futuristic lunar landers, powered by their solar-paneled exterior walls.

"These must be our cabins," observed Jake. "Pretty cool."

"Totally," said Kojo. "If NASA made mini-Winnebagos, that's what they'd look like."

Finally, the limo's privacy shield scrolled down.

"Welcome to Genius Camp, gentlemen," said the driver. "I hope you enjoy your stay."

"Thanks, man," said Kojo.

"Stay smart," said the driver.

"Huh?" said Jake.

"That's the Zinkle company motto," explained the driver. "Stay smart."

"Well," said Kojo, "we're sure gonna try, baby."

20

Jake and Kojo climbed out of the limo bus.

While they were busy with their bags, four kids, all of them about the same age as Jake and Kojo, ventured out to the miniature front porches of their high-tech camp cabins.

Three of them were wearing Genius Camp baseball caps, Z-shirts, and cargo shorts. The fourth was wearing a hijab and jeans. They all squinted at Jake and Kojo, sizing up the new arrivals. One kid—a guy with close-cropped orangish hair—was even using a small pair of binoculars.

"Must be the other geniuses," Jake whispered to Kojo. "Our competition."

Another bungalow door whooshed open, the way they do at a supermarket, and Christina, the tech exec, now with a whistle lanyard around her neck, came marching out of her tiny house, carrying a tablet computer.

"Welcome, Jake and Kojo. I trust your trip up from the city was uneventful?"

"Uh, yeah," said Jake. He saw no need to mention Haazim Farooqi's potential jelly bean breakthrough.

"Love the moat," said Kojo. "What time do you feed the crocodiles?"

Jake chuckled. Nobody else cracked a grin. Not Christina. Not the four other junior geniuses. In fact, one girl (she had her camp cap on backward) rolled her eyes.

"For the next week," Christina continued as if Kojo had never spoken, "I will be your camp counselor and these will be your homes. Before you settle in, please allow me to introduce you to the other campers, all of whom have extremely high IQs."

"Higher than Jake's?" asked Kojo with a smirk.

Christina hesitated. "No."

"Boo-yah! Call off the competition. Jake rules, everybody else drools."

"Sounds good to me," said the girl who'd just rolled her eyes. "Because I totally don't want to waste my time at computer camp. By the way, I'm Dawn Yang. Maybe you read about me in *People* magazine? The next teen tycoon? My mother and father made me come to this camp because they said I needed a break. That I work too hard. That I'm too"—she made air quotes—" 'focused' on building my tech empire."

The boy with the orange hair raised his hand.

"Yes, Poindexter?" said Christina.

"In physics, a focus is the point at which rays of light, heat, or radiation meet after being refracted or reflected. You can also focus a telescope, but you can no longer purchase a Ford Focus, because they have discontinued making that model of automobile."

"Thank you, Poindexter," said the camp counselor. "Our next camper is Mackenzie Meekleman. She is a musical prodigy and, at age twelve, has already earned her PhD in French studies from Brown University."

A very shy girl, her camp Z-shirt rumpled, was hugging herself, staring down at her feet, and trying hard to disappear.

She mumbled something. Very softly. It might've been "Hello." Could've been "Goodbye." Could've been "Rutabaga."

"And, finally, from Boston, Abia Sulayman."

Abia, the girl wearing a hijab, glared at Jake.

"Meeting you reminds me of when I first met Kyle Keeley," she said.

"Whoa," said Kojo. "The kid from Ohio who wins all those Lemoncello games on TV and stuff?"

"Indeed," said the girl. "He and I competed in Mr. Lemoncello's Library Olympics and then teamed up together for the Great Library Race."

"Cool!" said Jake.

"Yes. Now. However, when I first met him, Kyle Keeley was very much like you, Jake McQuade. An arrogant, boastful show-off."

"Whoa," said Jake, defensively raising both hands, "that's not me."

"Oh, really?" scoffed Abia. "I've seen those YouTube videos. The ones where you sink three-pointers from half-court."

"Aw, he was just showing off," said Kojo, not realizing he'd just proven the girl's point.

Jake felt slightly ashamed of himself. Abia didn't know the real Jake McQuade. Just the flashy, show-offy one from YouTube. But she had been absolutely correct in her instant analysis of Jake McQuade's public image.

Probably because Abia Sulayman's genius didn't come from jelly beans.

21

Jake and Kojo each got their own tiny-house cabin at opposite ends of the half circle.

Kojo's cabin was between Poindexter Perkins's and Dawn Yang's.

"Would you like one of my business cards?" Dawn asked Kojo.

"Whoa. You have business cards?"

"Uh, yeah."

"Me too."

"What's your slogan?" asked Dawn, flicking Kojo a sleek rectangle of shiny plastic. "Mine is 'Yang Tech: The Dawn of a New Day.'"

"Because your first name is Dawn?"

"Uh, yeah."

Kojo slid his slim stack of business cards back into his pants pocket.

"I'm, uh, still working on my slogan. Focus-grouping a bunch of 'em to see which one sings the loudest."

"Cool," said Dawn. Her phone chirped. "Excuse me, Kojo. Gotta run. This is my CFO. Chief financial officer."

"Yeah. I'm thinking about getting one of those, too."

Dawn hurried into her cabin.

"These sleep units are extremely well designed," blurted Poindexter, standing on the porch outside his cabin. "The solar panels on the slanted roof make them very energy efficient. Plus the housekeepers put a chocolate-dipped marshmallow on your pillow every night after they fluff it. The pillow, not the marshmallow. Although I do like Marshmallow Fluff. Especially with peanut butter. How about you?"

Kojo was too stunned to answer the marshmallow question.

"There are housekeepers? I thought this was supposed to be camp."

"It is! But it's Genius Camp. So everything's a whole lot smarter. That's why there are no latrines. We each have our own high-tech super toilet!"

"Oh, joy," said Kojo. He hauled his duffel into his cabin.

Meanwhile, at the far end of the circle, Jake dragged his long green bag up the steps of his ultramodern cabin. The front door automatically slid open. Jake stepped inside.

"Welcome, Jake McQuade," said a six-inch-tall rubbery polar bear sculpture. It was basically the shape of a mango with two black dots for eyes, a rounded trapezoid for a nose, and two tiny triangles up top for ears. The polar bear had a soothing female voice. The belly of its white body fluctuated through a rainbow of colors generated by internal LEDs. "I'm Lulu."

"Oh, you're like Alexa or Siri?"

"That is correct. Might I show you around your bungalow?"

"Um, sure, Lulu."

"May I suggest the energizer environmental mood?"

"Fine. Knock yourself out."

Peppy music wafted out of hidden speakers. The light inside the modular unit became warm and golden. Jake even smelled fresh-squeezed orange juice.

Mood set, the home assistant gave Jake an audio tour of his temporary 325-square-foot modular home. The place had everything. Video monitors that rose up out of furniture. Another screen that lowered from the ceiling so you could watch stuff in bed. A clean and efficient bathroom with a glass shower stall and a toilet that did things Jake really didn't want done.

There was a bed hidden inside the sofa—but it wasn't the usual sofa bed with a steel bar that pinched your spine. This bed silently slid out from under the couch. When it did, Jake noticed a pair of plastic-wrapped chocolate marshmallows nestled on the satiny pillow.

"Please be sure to take those to the opening night campfire," said Lulu. "They are a more efficient, smarter way to make s'mores—no need for separate marshmallows and chocolate bars."

Jake picked up the shrink-wrapped treats and tucked them into the hip pocket of his cargo shorts.

"Would you like me to close your bed?" asked Lulu.

"Sure. Great idea."

Jake heard a *whoosh* and a whir. The bed retracted itself into the couch. It was as if Transformers became furniture instead of cars or alien monsters. Jake strolled to the front door, which sensed his approach and, once again, slid sideways for him.

Abia Sulayman was on the front porch of the neighboring cabana. She popped a chocolate-covered marshmallow into her mouth.

"Are you ready for the first challenge?" she asked, confidently licking melted chocolate off her fingertips, one digit at a time.

"Sure. What's the challenge?"

"A twilight nature hike. We have to walk half a mile to the opening campfire ceremonies. There will be brain-boggling questions along the way. You must answer them before moving on. First one to the campfire wins the opening round."

"Oh. So it's like a game?"

"No. It is an intellectual challenge." Abia popped open the tight balloon of clear plastic covering another chocolate-dipped marshmallow and chucked the spongy glob into her mouth.

"You really like those, huh?"

"Yes. I find them to be an efficient snacking delivery system. And I checked with Christina. They are halal. Permissible."

Jake pulled out the two plastic-wrapped marshmallows he'd found on his pillow. "Here. Have mine. I can't stand marshmallows."

Abia arched a skeptical eyebrow. "And why is that?"

"Peeps. I was six. Maybe I ate too many. Maybe I ate a whole carton. Maybe I ate two cartons. And maybe I painted the toilet bowl bright pink, yellow, and blue, if you catch my drift."

"You greedily overconsumed and regurgitated."

"Yeah. Here."

He tossed Abia the two plastic-wrapped marshmallows. She caught them one-handed without flinching.

"Thank you," she said. "But I will not be bribed, Jake McQuade. I will not go easy on you during the upcoming nature hike competition."

"Understood," said Jake.

The brainy Bostonian might've slightly softened, but Jake realized Abia Sulayman would never become as squishy as a marshmallow.

Instead, she'd probably harden into his toughest competitor.

22

Christina gave each of the campers a zPad tablet computer when they gathered for the nature hike.

"Do we get to keep this?" asked Jake.

"Of course. You'll need it throughout your camping experience."

"Awesome," said Kojo. "You guys give out good swag."

Christina ignored him. Again.

"Please turn your attention to your screens. Mr. Zinkle will now officially welcome you to Genius Camp."

All the campers stared down at their tablets. Zane Zinkle's face appeared. He was sitting in a very white office, smiling like a jack-o'-lantern and sliding his glasses with his pinky. Again.

"Nose pads, baby," muttered Kojo. "Nose pads."

"Welcome, officially, to Genius Camp," said Zinkle.

"I hope you boys and girls enjoy your time with us this week as well as all the . . ."

He smirked.

"All the 'mental challenges' we have planned for you."

Then he giggled.

"We're looking for the best and the brightest children in the land, and right now that is you. We'll see where things stand at the end of the week."

Another giggle.

Kojo and Jake exchanged a quizzical look.

"Remember, here at Zinkle, smart is good, but smartest is best. There can, of course, be only one 'smartest.' Such is the nature of superlative adjectives. Just ask your English teachers when you go home. So, welcome to camp. Nature's way of feeding mosquitoes. Christina?"

Zinkle's image vanished from the tablet screens.

The camp counselor gestured to a woodsy hiking trail.

"You will find three puzzles along the path to the campfire circle," she announced. "You must solve each one before moving on. The questions will be displayed on screens; you will enter answers on your tablet, which will let you know if you have answered correctly. Once you reach the campfire, feel free to help yourselves to all the chocolate-covered marshmallows and graham crackers you desire and proceed to make . . ." She read the next bit off a note card. " 'Ooey-gooey, chocolatey, chewy s'mores.' The first one to arrive at the finish line will earn the first ten points to be awarded here at Genius Camp.

The second finisher will receive eight points, the third six, and so on."

Poindexter raised his hand.

"Yes?" said Christina.

"Following your mathematical equation to its logical conclusion, Camp Counselor Christina—which, by the way, is an excellent example of alliteration: the occurrence of the same letter or sound at the beginning of adjacent or closely connected words—the last person to the designated terminus of this exercise will receive zero points. Am I correct?"

"Uh, yeah," said Dawn. "But guess what: we all figured it out for ourselves because we're all geniuses. Plus I'm fifteen. So there's that."

"Eye of newt dancer," mumbled Mackenzie. Or she might've said, "Hi, nuke disaster." Maybe even "I knew the answer." Jake couldn't understand a word she muttered.

"Might we proceed?" asked Abia. "I am eager to earn my first ten points."

"Your puzzles await," declared Christina. She pulled out a stopwatch. "Go!"

23

The six campers scurried up the trail as nimbly as they could. None of the other geniuses were quite as athletic as Jake and Kojo.

Running as if they were executing a fast break in a basketball game, Jake and Kojo easily took a fifty-yard lead. They soon discovered the first quiz screen glowing on a post near a picnic table. It was a picture puzzle:

WHERE IS THE SPY HIDING?

It took Kojo one second to figure out the answer.

"Simple, baby!" He tapped the screen of his zPad. It gave him a pleasant victory chime.

Jake was maybe a half second behind Kojo. The graphic showed three cars parked in driveways at houses labeled *A, B,* and *C.* Only the car parked in front of house A had its nose pointed toward the road, ready to make a quick getaway without backing up. *A* had to be the answer.

Jake tapped *A*. His pleasant chime started the instant Kojo's finished.

"Come on," said Kojo. "Let's find the second puzzle. And next time, don't make me wait so long while you figure out the answer."

Jake laughed. "I was half a nanosecond behind you."

"Technically incorrect," said Kojo as the two friends jogged up the trail. "A nanosecond is one-billionth of a second."

"I stand corrected," said Jake, risking a look over his shoulder. The others had finally made it to the first puzzle.

Mackenzie's zPad was already chiming.

"Second screen!" shouted Jake, pointing to a glowing rectangle on a pole near an evergreen.

"Bring it on!" said Kojo, who was pumped after the first brainteaser had been so easy.

The second screen presented a riddle:

WHAT TYPE OF CHEESE IS MADE BACKWARD?

Jake knew the answer immediately. Kojo, not so much.

"Oh, man," he groaned.

"You want a hint?" Jake whispered.

"No," Kojo whispered back. "I want to figure it out."

"I already did."

"Because you ate that culinary cuisine bean," hissed Kojo.

"It's—"

"Don't tell me, Jake. Here comes Abia Sulayman. She's going to be your main competition. You've got to beat her, baby."

"Okay, okay."

"I'll try to slow her down. Go! I've got your back."

Jake tapped *E-D-A-M* on his zPad's simulated keyboard because Edam cheese was *made* spelled backward. He heard another pleasant chime confirm that he was correct, and he hurried up the trail. Behind him, he could hear Kojo babbling.

"When I make cheese," Kojo was saying, "the first thing I do is milk a few cows. . . ."

"This is a simple word puzzle," Jake heard Abia huff. "A child could solve it."

"Well, technically," said Kojo, "we *are* children."

"Speak for yourself."

As Jake searched for the third puzzle, he could hear Abia's "correct answer" chime ringing behind him.

Jake ran faster. He was breathing hard. Abia was on his tail. She could really move when she wanted to.

Jake came to the third screen. The final brainteaser was another visual puzzle.

WHAT IS THE NUMBER OF THE PARKING SPOT?

Jake immediately knew the answer.

87!

All you had to do was flip the image over in your brain. *98* became *86*. *88* was *88*. *68* became *89*, and so on. The car was parked in space 87!

He typed in the number.

His zPad once again confirmed that he was correct. He took off running for the campfire circle just as Abia started reading the third screen.

He'd done it!

He made it to the finish before anyone else. He'd scored the first ten points. He could also help himself to a mountain of plastic-wrapped chocolate-dipped marshmallows piled high inside a brightly colored wicker basket with a handle.

It looked like an Easter basket.

An Easter basket filled with cleverly disguised Peeps.

Jake's stomach clenched. His shoulders involuntarily hunched. His hand flew to his mouth.

It took everything he had not to hurl.

24

Jake and Kojo didn't do so well in the next competition.

As the sun sank into the lake, Camp Counselor Christina led the six genius campers down to a wooden dock.

"Before our campfire ceremonies commence," she said, "we'd like to test your nautical and coding skills with a regatta of remote-controlled sailboats. There is a third-party app called *Regatta* on your zPad. It will allow you to write computer code that will manipulate your boat's rudder and sail trim as you weave your way through the buoys, which are arranged in a classic Olympic triangle course configuration."

"Excuse me?" said Abia, raising her hand. "What does playing with a toy sailboat have to do with measuring our superior intelligence?"

"Uh, tons," said Dawn. "Churning out code to sail with nothing but wind power provides an excellent series of computer programming challenges, not to mention real-world physics problems."

"In other words," said Kojo, cocking an eyebrow, "you've got one of these toy boats at home?"

"A few," said Dawn. "They're left over from when I wrote the *Regatta* app."

"This is your app?" said Jake with an admiring grin. Dawn shrugged.

Needless to say, she won the sunset regatta competition.

Poindexter came in second and supplied the other campers with a nonstop running commentary of his every move.

"As you can see, the wind, even though it is blowing from the side, is propelling my craft forward due to the well-known principle of aerodynamic lift."

Jake came in third because, thanks to Farooqi's jelly beans, he was a pretty good coder and computed a formula to account for lift, drag, and all the other forces acting on the miniature sailboat.

Sailboat challenge completed, Christina led everybody back to the campfire and invited Mackenzie Meekleman to "lead us in tonight's singalong."

"Guy avenue pea haired eaten," Mackenzie mumbled.

Or at least that's what Jake heard. It could've been "Iambic free pair Annie wing." Or, most likely, "I haven't prepared anything." Mackenzie spoke the way Jake's phone sometimes garbled his dictation.

Christina insisted.

And Mackenzie surprised everybody by belting out, in a loud voice (with perfect diction), a complicated patter song from a Gilbert and Sullivan operetta called *The Mikado*.

"To sit in solemn silence in a dull, dark dock,
In a pestilential prison, with a life-long lock,
Awaiting the sensation of a short, sharp shock,
From a cheap and chippy chopper on a big black block!"

She was awarded ten points because nobody else could sing. Well, Kojo could rap, but Camp Counselor Christina "wasn't interested."

"Here at Genius Camp," she told him, "we focus on the classics of the musical canon."

"Rap is classical," Kojo insisted. "It's poetry. Come on, it's right there in the name. Rhythm and Poetry. *R-A-P!*"

"Did you know," said Poindexter, "that the cannon, a metal projectile-firing weapon, first appeared in China sometime during the twelfth or thirteenth century, replacing an earlier gunpowder weapon called the fire lance?"

"Thank you, Poindexter," said Christina, cutting him off before he could bore all the other campers to sleep.

She had more work to do.

At the top of her list was passing around the chocolate-covered marshmallows, which, much to her delight, Mackenzie, Dawn, Poindexter, and Abia all gobbled down greedily—even before they grabbed any graham crackers.

25

Zane Zinkle sat in his domed office studying the array of two dozen video monitors livestreaming the action at Genius Camp.

The grounds of the Zinkleplex campus were filled with hidden surveillance cameras. The things were everywhere. But tonight Zinkle was focused on the action at the nature trail, the lake, and the campfire.

"Christina continues to do an adequate job equal to her level of competence," he dictated to the Lulu bear on his desk. "Baseline parameters for the primary targets will have been established and recorded within the next hour. Lulu?"

"Yes, Mr. Zinkle?"

"Please give me an update on the Riverview Middle School test market."

"All is as it should be."

Virtuoso, with its incredible speed and massive storage capacity, was handling the much larger, much more complex operation in the city.

"I am currently tracking data points on all five hundred and twenty-seven program participants," reported the virtual assistant. "You are well positioned to increase Zinkle Inc.'s profitability."

"Excellent."

He stuck out his tongue at a magazine cover labeling his company the *Second-Wealthiest in the World*.

He returned to dictating his voice memo.

"Operation Brain Drain is poised to move on to its second phase—here at the camp as well as at our adopted school. If all goes as anticipated—and it usually does when I am the one anticipating it—both techniques will yield the tools needed to broaden our scope and achieve our double objectives!"

He laughed maniacally for a full minute.

When he was finished, Lulu asked if he would like her to adjust the lighting for a "more celebratory mood."

"Not yet, Lulu," replied Zinkle. "But soon."

26

Dinner around the campfire was delicious and prepared by gourmet chefs.

And, of course, there were s'mores for dessert.

"Pass," said Jake, tasting something nasty in the back of his throat the instant he smelled the syrupy scent of the marshmallow Dawn just freed from its crinkly plastic bag.

"What's with you and marshmallows, man?" asked Kojo, who was seated to his left.

"Long story."

"Was there chunk-blowing involved? A chow shower? Doing the hokey croaky? A gastro geyser from Barfalo Bill and your cousin Ralph?"

Jake nodded. And suppressed a vurp—a very vomity burp.

"Pass!" said Kojo when a waiter in camp khakis

offered him the silver tray filled with chocolate-dipped marshmallows. All the others were skewering the soft and spongy sugar pillows and toasting them over the open fire.

"The melting point of chocolate is between eighty-six and ninety degrees Fahrenheit, or a peak of thirty-two degrees Celsius," Poindexter alerted anybody who might be interested (which turned out to be nobody).

"This is not the best method for producing s'mores," said Abia, popping a cold marshmallow into her mouth. "The melted chocolate will drip off before the covered confection can become crispy on the outside, gooey on the inside."

"Well, I'm sure Mr. Zinkle thought of that," said Poindexter. "He's always so attentive to the scientific literature of any subject—the details *and* the data."

"Are you always such a sycophantic bootlicker?" asked Abia.

"I beg your pardon?"

Dawn poked at the fire with a stick. "She means a brownnoser, lickspittle, or toady."

"Pie octuplet all Freddy smelled dead," muttered Mackenzie, who, it seemed, only had perfect diction when she sang. But Jake was getting better at translating her muffled sentences, even the ones further muddied by the mushy mound of marshmallow mashed inside her mouth. Judging from the brown goop dribbling off the end of her skewer, Mackenzie had to be saying, "My chocolate already melted."

"All right, campers," announced Christina. "It's time for our literary salon."

"Excuse me?" said Abia.

"Campfire stories."

"Oh!" said Kojo. "I've got a good one."

"Not the one about the coffin," Jake whispered out of the side of his mouth.

"That's the one, baby. It's a campfire classic!"

Jake rolled his eyes.

Kojo loved the coffin story.

Jake?

Not so much.

27

Abia went first.

She launched into a Somali folktale about a hyena and a fox.

"Bari ayaa dawaco adhi fara badan ka cuni jirtay reero meel deggan," she said in Somali.

Which Jake couldn't help auto-translating. Out loud. "Once upon a time a fox was eating sheep from a stable."

Abia turned to him. "These stories were passed down orally by my Somali ancestors for many generations, Jake McQuade. It is important that they be told in Somali first. I will translate, more correctly than you, once I finish telling the tale as it was originally intended."

Jake felt terrible. "Sorry. I was just trying to help out."

"No. You were just showing off. Again."

"You *were* hotdogging a little, bro," whispered Kojo.

Jake held up his hands. "I'm sorry. It won't happen again. I promise."

Abia continued her tale.

Jake was the only one (other than Abia, of course) who understood the story the first time through. A fox was caught stealing sheep. A bunch of angry shepherds tied the fox to a tree and went off in search of firewood. The fox would be tossed into blazing flames for his crimes.

The fire crackling in front of Abia made her story even better.

In the end, though, the clever fox tricked a super-greedy (and not-so-smart) hyena into taking his place. So the angry shepherds tossed the hyena into the fire instead of the fox. The end.

The lesson? You will be punished if you are ignorant and greedy.

When Abia finished telling the story in Somali, she told it again. This time in English.

When she reached the big finish (the second time Jake was hearing it), she looked directly at Jake. "The greedy and foolish hyena died in the fire."

The campfire popped and sent up a shower of glowing red embers. Everybody applauded. More individually wrapped marshmallows were passed around.

During the brief break, Kojo turned to whisper to Jake. "Whoa. Abia Sulayman does not like you, bro."

"Yeah."

"You're the greedy and foolish hyena."

"No, I'm not."

"Ha! Good luck convincing her."

28

Kojo was up next.

He stood and dusted off his shorts.

"Okay, people," he said. "My turn. This is the real deal. A campfire ghost story. On a cold and windy night, not unlike tonight—"

"Actually," said Poindexter, "I find the temperature to be quite moderate this evening."

"Because you're sitting next to a fire. Work with me. Now, then—on this particular cold and windy night, a man was walking home alone down a dark, deserted street that ran past the local cemetery."

"Well, that wasn't very smart," said Dawn. "Hasn't this dude ever seen a movie? Dark, deserted streets near cemeteries are where scary things happen all the time. His probability of danger just increased exponentially."

"Was it the shortest route?" asked Abia.

"Yes!" said Kojo. "It was the shortest route, so he had to take it. Because of geometry."

Jake was only half listening. He was still smarting from Abia calling him a hyena. Thanks to some of the stuff in one of Farooqi's jelly beans, Jake knew that the fools in Somali allegorical animal tales were always hyenas. Or donkeys.

Abia thought Jake was a greedy fool. A selfish clown.

Kojo reached the part in his ghost story where a coffin rises up out of the graveyard and, "BUMP, BUMP, BUMP," it chases after the man.

"But how can the coffin propel itself?" asked Poindexter.

"It has no wheels or other means of locomotion," added Dawn.

"Fish dish repickle us," muttered Mackenzie, which Jake quickly translated to "This is ridiculous."

Jake felt sorry for Kojo. It was practically impossible to tell a fantastical piece of fiction to these superlogical eggheads.

"Doesn't matter how it moved," said Kojo, plowing ahead. "But it kept on coming. The man ran for his life. He saw a broken tree branch on the ground. He grabbed it. Tossed it over his shoulder at the coffin—but it just splintered when it hit the coffin, and the coffin kept coming. Faster—BUMPITY, BUMPITY, BUMPITY!"

"Did the man think to call nine-one-one?" asked

Poindexter. "That's what any reasonable person would do in such a predicament."

"He had a phone," said Kojo, improvising fast. "But he threw that at the coffin, too."

"I hope he had a full-replacement insurance policy," said Abia.

Dawn shook her head. "Nah. Trust me: insurance won't cover phones you intentionally throw away."

Abia nodded. "True. Very good point, Dawn."

"Yeah. Been there, done that."

"It doesn't matter!" said Kojo, sounding irritated. "The cell phone didn't stop the coffin, either. The coffin kept coming. The man got home. Saw his splitting ax leaning up against the woodpile . . ."

"He uses an ax to split wood?" said Poindexter. "An ax is ideal for *chopping* wood, but a maul, with its heavier and thicker, wedge-shaped head and slight convexity, is better for *splitting* it."

"He had both! Okay? And he threw them both at the coffin. Then he threw his chain saw and his hydraulic wood splitter. They all bounced off. The coffin wouldn't stop."

Abia crossed her arms over her chest. "I suspect the protagonist of your story now regrets disposing of his cell phone in such a foolhardy fashion."

"Doesn't matter!" Kojo said again. "He ran into his house, hurried up the stairs, grabbed his shotgun, turned around, and blasted the coffin with both barrels. But the buckshot bounced harmlessly off the coffin as it climbed up the stairs—BUMP, CLOMP, BUMP, CLOMP!"

"The logic of this tale escapes me," said Poindexter. "How can a coffin climb steps? How can metal bullets bounce off a wooden coffin?"

"It was a steel coffin!" said Kojo, practically screaming. "Anyway, once he was upstairs, the man jumped into the bathroom and locked the door—even though he knew it wouldn't do any good. Nothing could stop the coffin. It banged against the door. Once. Twice. On the third try, the door splintered and the coffin lurched forward. Frantic, the man grabbed the first thing he could find. A bottle of cough syrup. He threw it at the coffin. The bottle shattered. Cough syrup dribbled down the front of the coffin. And, just like that, the coffin stopped."

Jake closed his eyes and shook his head.

He couldn't believe that Kojo had told that corny story. Again.

The other campers tilted their heads like puppies who don't quite understand what their human is saying.

The fire snapped, sputtered, and crackled.

"I doughnut Gidget," mumbled Mackenzie.

"Huh?" said Kojo.

"She doesn't get it," Jake explained.

"Then she wasn't paying attention!" screeched Kojo. "The cough syrup stopped the coffin! Nothing else would."

Jake tried to explain the jokey ghost story's punch line

to the confused genius campers. "The man stopped the coffin with cough syrup."

Still no reaction. Just more crackling and snapping and popping from the fire.

And crickets.

Jake could hear crickets, too.

"Ohhhh," said Dawn. "It's a homophone. *Coughin'* and *coffin* sound alike but have different meanings and different spellings."

"Exactly!" said Kojo. "It's a homophone."

"I thought he threw away his phone," said Abia, tossing yet another chocolate-dipped marshmallow into her mouth. Mackenzie giggled and popped in two.

"Does anyone else have a story they'd like to tell?" asked Christina.

Dawn raised her hand. "I'd like to tell you all the origin story behind Yang Tech. 'The Dawn of a New Day.' "

"Um, Christina?" said Jake. "Kojo and I have to leave."

"Yeah," grumped Kojo. "It's past our bedtime."

"No problem," said Dawn. "I'll leave you guys a copy of my story outside your cabin doors. My PR team had several dozen printed before I left home."

"Thanks," said Jake. "Come on, Kojo. Let's go to our cabins and push all those buttons on the high-tech toilets."

"Good idea," said Kojo. As they walked away, he

added, "I should've said 'cough drop' instead of 'cough syrup.'"

"Maybe," said Jake.

"Next time, I'll say 'cough drop.'"

Jake patted his best friend gently on the back. "Yeah. 'Cough drop' might be better."

29

The next morning, the six campers met their "new counselor," a peppy guy named Todd.

"Gooooood morning, geniuses!" he hollered when he came into the dining hall, where everybody was plastic-spooning soggy oatmeal out of flimsy paper bowls. "Christina has been called away. Mr. Z needs her for a training seminar. Anywho, I'm your new counselor, Todd Binkley. And, yes, I really look this good this early in the morning."

Poindexter raised his hand.

"Oooh," said Todd. "My first question. Hit me up, Carrot Top."

"My name is Poindexter Perkins."

"I know, Red. It's on my clipboard." Todd showed everybody his clipboard. "What's on your mind, Red?"

"Why is the food so terrible this morning?"

"Zits boat mule dish babs zoo tootly dish guts cling," mumbled Mackenzie.

"I agree," said Kojo, who was also getting used to Mackenzie's muffled speech. "This oatmeal is absolutely disgusting."

"Sorry, kids," said Todd. "Today's the chef's day off. So I just nuked some instant oatmeal in the microwave. Who got the apples and cinnamon?"

Abia and Mackenzie both raised their hands.

"But," said Abia, "I question if these are real apples or merely a reconstituted chemical concoction consisting of calcium carbonate, sulfur dioxide, riboflavin, and guar gum."

"Oooh. Good question. Wish I had the answer. But I flunked Oatmeal 101 when I was in college. Heh-heh-heh. I'm kidding. I never studied oatmeal or any other cereal in college. Kind of wish I had. Froot Loops are fascinating. Oh-kay." He checked his clipboard. "Today is crafts day."

"Will we be designing and crafting our own apps?" asked Dawn.

Todd shook his head.

"I'd like to celebrate the vibrant cultures of the ancient world by exploring textile painting," said Abia.

"Whoosh!" Todd brushed a hand over his head. "That is way above my pay grade, little lady. Let's stick to twenty-first-century crafts."

"I am not a little lady," said Abia.

"Riiiiight." Todd flashed his smile. "You're a little genius lady."

"How about computer coding?" said Poindexter.

"That's a twenty-first-century craft. As is constructing Lego models of various *Star Wars* vessels."

"Nope," said Todd. "I'm thinking Popsicle sticks and wood glue, and everybody gets fifty points just for trying."

"Seriously?" said Abia.

"You betcha! Come on, gang. Put down your bowls and follow me!" He tooted on his whistle, which was attached to a very colorful lanyard. "Let's get artsy-fartsy and crafty-wafty! Heh-heh-heh."

All six campers rolled their eyes. But they did follow the way-too-happy Todd out of the dining hall and into the woods. The new counselor marched along the path with a drum major's exaggerated stork walk. He also sang a goofy camp song.

> *"Barfonyou, Barfonyou, Barfonyou.*
> *In Russian that means that I love you. . . ."*

"That is incorrect," said Poindexter. "The Russian expression for 'I love you' would be 'Ya tebya lyublyu.'"

Todd kept singing and didn't miss a beat.

> *"If I had it my way*
> *I'd Barfonyou all daaaay.*
> *Barfonyou, Barfonyou, Barfonyou."*

"Your song is based on a faulty premise, sir," shouted Abia. "That is not the correct Russian phraseology!"

"Who cares?" said Todd. "'Barfonyou' is funnier."

"It is," giggled Mackenzie. "'Barfonyou' is funny."

Jake looked at Kojo, who was looking at him. They were both shocked and surprised.

"She doesn't mumble anymore?" said Kojo.

Jake shrugged. "Must've been something in the oatmeal."

"Yeah. All those artificial apples."

30

"Okay, campers, craft away!" said Todd when they reached the Arts and Crafts Center, which wasn't a cool high-tech anything.

It was a screened-in picnic pavilion with a cracked concrete floor. A dozen wooden picnic tables were spaced out under the aluminum shed roof. Many of them were covered with newspapers to catch any glue splatters. There were also plastic bowls overflowing with plastic-wrapped chocolate marshmallows.

"Here are the Popsicle sticks," announced Todd, pointing to a mountain of the thin, rounded-tip pieces of wood stacked inside a pair of blue bins. "There're glue bottles on that shelf thingy over there."

Even though Todd was addressing the campers, he was actually talking to the face of his phone. His thumbs were busily tapping out a text or playing a video game or calling up an app.

"Have fun, you guys," he said to his phone and any-body else within earshot. "This is your only activity until lunch, which is at noon. So, uh, that's only like four hours from now because it's already nine-fifteen."

All the campers except Mackenzie shared a look.

"Um, Todd?" said Dawn. "Don't mean to bust your chops, dude, but if it's nine-fifteen, then noon is only, like, two hours and forty-five minutes away."

"Awesome. Guess lunch will be early today. Okay, glue your sticks, kids. I'm just gonna chill and Tweedle."

"What's Tweedle?" asked Mackenzie, who had appar-ently lost all the mumble marbles in her mouth.

"Incredible new app for the zPhone," said Todd.

"Never heard of it," said Dawn.

"It's kind of like a hipper version of TikTok," Todd explained. "Totally immersive and interactive. Tweedle shows you all the moves to make."

Todd wedged his zPhone in the gap between planks on a tabletop. He tapped a button on the phone screen, backed up several paces, and waited for the phone to show him what to do. And then he started doing it.

Mackenzie seemed fascinated. Mesmerized, even.

"Can I Tweedle?" she asked.

"Sure," said Todd. "The app is preloaded on every zPhone."

"Awesomesauce!"

While Mackenzie fiddled with her phone—and mind-lessly unwrapped and munched more marshmallows—

Kojo and Jake grabbed a few handfuls of Popsicle sticks and sat down at an empty table.

"This place is weird," said Kojo.

Jake agreed. "And getting weirder all the time."

"What do you want to make?"

"I dunno."

Abia was at a nearby table.

"I'm going to construct a replica of the Fakr ad-Din Mosque," she announced. "The oldest mosque in Mogadishu."

"You're going to build it with Popsicle sticks?" said Kojo skeptically.

She nodded. "And glue."

"Wouldn't it be easier just to make a flowerpot holder?" said Kojo. "Maybe a funny Popsicle stick penguin?"

"I prefer something a little more challenging."

"Need any help?" asked Jake.

"Yeah," said Kojo. "Let's make it a team project."

Abia gave Jake and Kojo a look. "What do you two know about the Fakr ad-Din Mosque?"

"Jake?" said Kojo. "You want to field this one?"

"Sure," said Jake. "It was built by the first sultan of Mogadishu in the twelve hundreds, following a right rectangular plan with a domed mihrab axis as well as a lofty prayer hall. Its use of conical vaults might be difficult for us to re-create with Popsicle sticks, but I'm pretty sure we can pull it off. We could start with the three entrance doors and try to re-create the ornate floral pattern on the central door with a Sharpie or ballpoint pen."

"Let's go with the ballpoint," suggested Kojo. "That way, we can kind of inscribe the wood—dig little gouges."

Dumbfounded, all Abia could do was nod in agreement.

Two and a half hours later, Abia, Jake, and Kojo completed their amazingly accurate scale model.

"I'm surprised you know so much about early African architecture, Jake McQuade," remarked Abia. She was actually smiling.

"Yeah," said Jake. "Me too."

The three mosque builders looked around the picnic pavilion to see what the other geniuses had created.

Poindexter had sculpted a wooden replica of Michelangelo's statue of David—except the head looked more like Zane Zinkle, complete with choppy bangs and round glasses.

Dawn had created a 3-D Popsicle stick model of the decision tree matrix for an app that could organize the user's sock drawer.

Meanwhile, Mackenzie and Todd were both dancing in front of their zPhones.

The lunch bell rang in the distance.

"Mr. Todd?" said Poindexter. "Mackenzie? It's time for lunch. You guys?"

Todd and Mackenzie remained oblivious. It was as if their dances had put them in a trance.

Jake jammed two fingers into his mouth and blew a screeching taxi-stopper of a whistle.

Todd and Mackenzie shook their heads. They looked dazed.

"You guys?" shouted Kojo. "Lunch!"

Todd nodded. "Cool."

Mackenzie nodded, too. "Totally."

Yep, thought Jake. *Things are definitely weird up here. And getting weirder.*

31

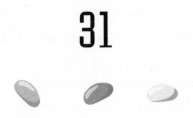

Lunch in the camp cafeteria was even worse than the breakfast food.

"Seriously?" said Kojo. "They have that whole kitchen and pantry back there, and all they're serving us is a pot of beans?"

"Well," said Jake, "according to the Bean Institute—"

"There's a Bean Institute?"

"Yep. And the website will tell you that beans are a 'simply delicious, naturally nutritious' food."

"Jake is correct," said Abia. "Beans, the pod-borne seeds of certain leguminous plants, are an inexpensive, simple-to-prepare, and healthy way to load up on fiber and plant-based protein."

"True," said Kojo. "They also give me gas."

"Beans, beans, the musical fruit!" said Todd with a chuckle. "The more you eat, the more you toot!"

"The more you toot," sang Mackenzie, "the better you'll feel!"

Todd leaned in to do harmony with Mackenzie on the last line.

"So eat your beans at every meal!"

They laughed and slapped each other a high five.

Abia dropped her jaw in horror. Poindexter gawped with disbelief. Dawn shook her head.

"Uh, you guys?" she said to Mackenzie and Todd. "This is supposed to be Genius Camp, not Fart Joke City."

"Agreed!" snapped Poindexter. "This is no place for rude, crude locker-room humor. Come on. Mr. Zinkle deserves better than that."

"I just think we deserve more lunch options," said Kojo, gesturing at the burbling pot of beans. "Maybe a PBJ. Even a granola bar would be better than this slop."

"Well," said Todd cheerfully, "you guys can always skip the main course and head straight to dessert." He gestured at another stack of those shrink-wrapped chocolate-coated marshmallows piled high on a cafeteria table.

And Jake vurped again. The things were everywhere.

"What's going on?" Kojo asked Todd. "Last night, we had all that gourmet cookout food. Those cheesy Mexican hot dogs with all the taco toppings were awesome. What happened to that chef?"

Todd shrugged. He also had a very blank and vapid expression on his face. "Don't know. Budget cuts?"

"Impossible!" said Poindexter. "Zane Zinkle is the

wealthiest billionaire in America. Maybe the world. He doesn't do 'budget cuts.'"

Abia moved to the dessert table, where she nervously unwrapped marshmallows and stuffed them, one by one, into her mouth. Dawn and Poindexter soon joined her. Mackenzie, while still fixated on her phone, was able to wolf down more marshmallows than any of them.

That's when Jake's phone played the theme song from *The Twilight Zone*—his ringtone for Haazim Farooqi.

Jake answered the call. "Hey there, Mr. Farooqi."

"Greetings, Subject One. How are things at Genius Camp?"

"Weird," said Jake.

"And getting weirder!" shouted Kojo in the background.

"I am sorry to hear that. I often feel the same way when attending Farooqi family functions here in New Jersey. Excuse me. I need to lower the gas on my Bunsen burner."

"Working on the jelly beans?"

"Not at the moment. Currently I am using it as a torch to caramelize my crème brûlée. I, of course, had to chill the custard before taking this caramelization step to ensure a thick and crackling crust."

Jake covered his phone with his hand. "He's still got mad culinary skills! The you-know-whats are working!"

"I am calling to let you know that I should soon have a complete batch of new jelly beans!" Farooqi declared.

"As well as several tasty dessert options. I'm moving on to molten lava cake next!"

Jake heard a beep. "Mr. Farooqi, thanks for the update. But I have to take this other call. It might be my mom or Emma."

"Very well, Subject One. Remember, your mind needs exercise, just like your body. That's why I think about jogging every day. Enjoy the rest of your Genius Camp brain-building activities."

That made Jake laugh a little. Because it seemed like, on the second day, Genius Camp had lost almost all of its smarts.

32

"It's Grace," Jake told Kojo after checking the caller ID.

"Aw, she misses her BF," said Kojo.

"How many times do I have to tell you, I am not her boyfriend." Jake tapped answer. "Hey, Grace."

"Hey. How are things at Genius Camp?"

"Extrañas," he said. "Y cada vez más extrañas."

"Strange? How so?"

"They have us playing with Popsicle sticks. I thought we'd be doing computer coding or applying creative thinking across multiple disciplines to solve real-world problems. And maybe some, you know, archery. They aren't even giving us points for anything anymore. I guess the competition is over."

"And you're not doing amazing things with Zane Zinkle?"

"Nope."

"Then he won't mind me yanking you out of there for a few hours. Guess what—the mayor has agreed to hear our pitch."

"For real?"

"Yep. She absolutely loved you on *Quiz Zone*. She's also very interested in my sneaker collection."

"So when does she want to see us?"

"Today. At four-thirty."

Jake glanced up at the wall clock. "It's almost one now."

"I know. That's why I'm sending a private helicopter to bring you guys back. It'll drop you off at school. We'll ride together to city hall with Uncle Charley."

Jake could hear the soft *thump-thump-thump* of an approaching helicopter.

"We have you near a clearing on the Zinkleplex campus, is that correct?" said Grace. "The dining hall?"

"Yeah, but how did—"

"You never should've given me permission to find and follow your phone, Jake," she said with a laugh. "I've been tracking you guys all morning."

"Well, I'm glad you did. See you soon."

"See you soon. Fly safe."

"We will. Although this time I think I'll let a real helicopter pilot handle the controls."

"Good idea. ¡Hasta luego!"

Jake tapped his screen and ended the call. The helicopter was landing in a field next to the dining hall.

"Come on, Kojo. That's our ride. Grace just sent us our own private shuttle."

"Where are we going?" asked Kojo.

"To the mayor's office!"

"The thing about the thing?" Kojo asked excitedly.

"Exactly."

"Let's roll, baby."

They both got up from the table.

"Um, Todd?" said Jake.

The camp counselor was still glued to his phone. He was doing some arm, hip, and chest thrusts, like he was in gym class.

"What's up, Jake-a-rino?"

"We're sorry but we need to—"

"Hang on. I'm about to Tweedle up to the next level."

"Congrats. Anyhow, Kojo and I need to take off."

"The mayor needs to see us at city hall," added Kojo.

"Awesome," said Todd.

The whirlybird's downdraft stirred up waves in the sea of green grass covering the manicured open field.

"Oh-kay," said Jake. "Please tell Mr. Zinkle we had to go back to the city. We'll catch up on any crafts projects we miss when we get back. Come on, Kojo. Let's go."

"I'm right behind you, baby."

The two friends hurried out of the dining hall.

"We'll be back," Jake shouted to Todd, who was oblivious to everything except whatever Tweedle was telling him to do next.

"He means we might be back," shouted Kojo. "We'll see. Taking it day by day."

"We have to come back, Kojo," Jake hollered as the two friends dashed toward the waiting helicopter. "We made a deal with Zinkle. If we don't return to Genius Camp, he'll take away everybody's free zPhones. We have to think about all the kids and teachers back home at Riverview Middle School."

"Oops."

"What?"

"I left my zPhone in my cabin."

"Me too."

"Okay," said Kojo. "Now we really do need to come back. I'm not using my zPhone, but those puppies cost three thousand dollars!"

They climbed into the helicopter and lifted off.

Jake wasn't sure, but as they cleared the treetops he thought he saw a silhouette standing in the windows of the flying-saucer-shaped penthouse on top of the Zinkle World Headquarters building.

It looked like it might be Zane Zinkle.

It also looked like he might be shaking his fist at the sky.

33

After the chopper landed on the Riverview Middle School baseball field, Principal Lyons drove Jake, Kojo, and Grace to city hall.

"I'm so proud of you three," he said. "You're using your incredible brains to do good in this world."

"Thanks," said Grace. "Luke Rawcliffe was a major player, too. I tried to find him so he could come, too, but he didn't return my text."

"Dude is good with his hands," said Kojo. "Knows his tools."

Jake grinned, remembering how Luke had saved his butt in tech ed. "That he does. . . ."

"I can't believe the mayor is actually going to listen to our pitch!" said Grace when they pulled into a parking space in front of the very impressive city hall.

"She has to," said Mr. Lyons. "You three are the most famous kids in town."

"True," said Kojo. "But, as they say in all those *Spider-Man* movies, with great fame comes great responsibility."

"Kojo?" said Jake. "Nobody ever said 'with great fame comes great responsibility' in a *Spider-Man* movie."

"Well, they should've."

The group was escorted up to the mayor's conference room. Mr. Green, the tech ed instructor, had already delivered the prototype of the very special recycling subway and bus pass dispenser his class had built. The machine, the size of a refrigerator, was standing at one end of a very long table.

Maria Modugno, the city's feisty mayor (and mega *Quiz Zone* fan), came into the meeting room with several members of her staff. She was wearing colorful sneakers.

"Goodness!" the mayor exclaimed when she saw the hulking box at the far end of her conference table. "What is that thing?"

"A reverse vending machine," said Jake proudly.

"Huh?"

"It doesn't pop out plastic bottles," said Kojo.

"Instead," said Grace, "it eats them and gives you money."

"Actually," said Jake, "it gives you a credit for your bus or subway fare."

"Brings a whole new meaning to 'paying with plastic,'" said Kojo. "See what I did there, Madam Mayor? 'Paying with plastic'?"

The mayor nodded. Her brow was furrowed. She was deep in thought.

"Save a nickel with one bottle," said Grace. "Or ride for free with forty."

"The solar panels on the sides will provide all the electricity a bus pass dispenser would need," said Jake. "For subway installations, we'd, of course, have to mount the power panels aboveground."

"Because that's where the sun shines, baby," explained Kojo.

"According to Greenpeace," said Jake, "there's up to twelve point seven million tons of plastic in our oceans."

"Because we're not doing enough to incentivize recycling," said Grace.

" 'Incentivize' means 'make people want to do something,' " added Kojo. "It was on our vocab test a couple weeks ago. I got an A-plus."

The mayor nodded. "I'm sure you did. You three are very bright. May I just say that I think it is quite commendable that you are all using your exceptional talents not for your own benefit but to do good in the world?"

"Well, ma'am," said Kojo, "with great fame comes great responsibility."

Jake and Grace rolled their eyes.

"And so?" said Mr. Lyons, holding up both hands as if asking the mayor to make a decision.

"You get a big yes from me!" said the mayor. "In fact, I want these bottle gobblers at every bus stop. Every subway station! And then I want vending machines that will only give you a bottle of soda if you give it one first!"

Mr. Lyons looked like he might burst with pride.

"This is brilliant," said the mayor. "You kids are brilliant!"

"Boo-yah!" cried the three friends. And then they fist-bumped.

34

Jake and Kojo decided not to head back to Genius Camp until the next morning.

"There aren't any real activities or anything," said Jake.

"Just lots of marshmallows and baked beans," added Kojo.

Grace laughed. "I'll contact the helicopter company. Tell them to pick you up at school tomorrow, say ten?"

They were all back in Mr. Lyons's car. He'd offered to chauffeur everybody home.

"Ten sounds great," said Jake. "Hey, you guys want to hang out at my house? We could order a pizza or something. Celebrate our vending-machine victory with my mom and Emma."

"I'm in," said Kojo.

Grace's zPhone buzzed. She glanced at the screen. "I, uh, can't," she said. "I have to do something."

Mr. Lyons pulled the car to a stop in front of Jake's apartment building. Now his zPhone was humming, too. He pulled it out of its dashboard holder and studied the screen.

"I have to do something, too," he said in a dull monotone.

"It's very important," droned Grace.

"Very, very important," echoed Mr. Lyons.

"Um, Mr. Lyons?" said Jake. "Grace? Are you guys okay?"

"Fine," said Grace.

"Never better," said Mr. Lyons. He sounded like he was sleepwalking.

"Seriously?" said Kojo. "Because you don't sound so good, sir."

"Heh-heh-heh," Mr. Lyons said dully. "It's just been a very long and exciting day."

"Very exciting," said Grace unexcitedly.

"Oh-kay," said Jake as he and Kojo climbed out of the car. "See you two at school tomorrow."

"And thanks for the whirlybird ride, Grace," added Kojo.

"Huh?" said Grace, sounding distracted.

"The whirlybird. The chopper."

Grace had a blank look on her face.

"The helicopter?" said Jake.

"Oh. Right. You're welcome."

Jake and Kojo stood on the sidewalk and watched the car pull away from the curb.

"So what's up with those two?" Kojo wondered out loud.

"I don't know," said Jake, sounding worried, maybe even alarmed. "It's like, all of a sudden, they were zombified. It reminded me of Mackenzie up at the camp."

"The mumbler?"

Jake nodded. "It seemed that she lost her mumble right before she started telling fart jokes."

"I noticed that, too."

"According to a very interesting article I read once—"

Kojo rolled his eyes. "Here we go again."

"This could be important, Kojo. A clue."

"Oh. In that case, lay it on me. I'm all about the clues."

"According to this fascinating piece by Julie Sedivy, mumbling isn't a sign of laziness. Sedivy writes, and I quote—"

"Of course you do."

" 'Dropping or reducing sounds displays an underlying logic similar to the data-compression schemes that are used to create MP3s and JPEGs.' Superintelligent people sometimes use mumbling, or, more precisely, phonetic reduction, to streamline their verbal output."

"It also made Mackenzie hard to understand."

"True. But then BOOM! She stopped mumbling. She also stopped sounding smart."

"So what dumbed her down?"

"I'm not sure." Jake nudged his head to where Mr. Lyons had parked his car for the drop-off. "But I have a hunch it might have something to do with her zPhone. She started staring at it the way Grace and Mr. Lyons were just now."

Kojo snapped his fingers. "Of course. It's a zPhone. 'Z' for 'zombie'!"

"Or 'Zinkle.'"

"Nah, they didn't turn into Zinkles, Jake. Their haircuts were still halfway decent."

Jake's eyes bugged out. "My mother has one of those phones. Well, actually, it's my sister's, but Mom took it."

It was Kojo's turn to panic. "My mom has one, too!"

35

"I gotta head upstairs!" said Jake.

"I need to run home," said Kojo. "Fast!"

"And we definitely need to be at school tomorrow. Every single student, teacher, and staff member has a zPhone."

"Yeah. Thanks to us. Well, actually, it's more thanks to you. I mean, if I'm being honest here, Jake, Zinkle wouldn't've invited me up to Genius Camp if I wasn't connected to you, so . . ."

"Kojo? Can we talk about who to blame later?"

"No need. I think we just covered it pretty thoroughly."

"Fine. Hurry home. Check on your folks. Keep in touch."

"Ten-four!"

Jake punched in the code for his apartment building's

security pad. The front door buzzed and unlocked. He dashed into the lobby and didn't waste time waiting for the elevator. He bounded up the steps in the stairwell.

He burst into his apartment. "Mom? Emma?"

Emma came running out of the kitchen. Panic filled her eyes.

"Jake! Thank goodness you're home!"

"Yeah. What's wrong?"

"Mom!" Emma sounded horrified. "She's in the kitchen. And, Jake? She's dancing! *Dancing!*"

Jake made a move toward the kitchen. Emma blocked him.

"No. You don't want to go in there. Once you see it, you can't unsee it." Emma did a bunny hop and some weird head and arm moves while pretending to be twirling an invisible Hula-Hoop around her hips.

"What's that?" Jake asked in horror.

"Mom's dance! She's doing whatever Tweedle tells her to."

"Tweedle? The free app on her zPhone?"

"Yep. It's all she does. She even skipped work today so she could 'Tweedle up' to the next level. We need to seriously limit her screen time, Jake. Maybe make her hand over the phone for the night one hour before bedtime."

Just then their mother meandered into the room. She looked dazed and slightly confused. Her zPhone was tightly gripped in her hand.

"Hello, Jake. I'm your mother. Michelle McQuade. That's my name."

"Mom? Are you feeling okay?"

She smiled a wan and feeble smile. "Never better, honey bunny."

"Mom?"

"Yes, Jakey-Wakey?"

"You sound weird."

"Would you like to see my Tweedle dance?"

"No!" Jake and Emma shouted together.

"We'll pass on the dance," said Jake. He tried to think of something to snap her out of whatever hypnotic trance she might be in. Maybe he could give her another task. "But I am kind of hungry."

Their mother blinked but didn't budge. "Oh. Okay."

Jake sniffed the air. It smelled bitter and a little smoky. "Um, what were you guys having for dinner?"

"Burnt tomato soup," muttered Emma.

"I'm sorry, honey," said Mom. "I didn't mean to burn the soup. I forgot that you have to take it off the hot thing."

"The stove?" said Jake.

"Yes! That's what they call it. The stove! Or the oven. It might be the oven. I get those two confused. Tell you what, kids. I'll pick up something at the grocery store. I need to go there anyway. We don't have any Pork Avenue Nacho Cheddar–Flavored Chicharrónes."

"Fried pork rinds?" said Emma. She looked like she might gag.

"Technically," said Jake, "they're not exactly the same. Pork rinds are the skin only, whereas chicharrónes are a thin cut of—"

"Who cares?" screamed Emma, tugging at her hair. "Mom's gone wacko."

"No," said their mother. "I've gone hog wild. For Pork Avenue Nacho Cheddar–Flavored Chicharrónes. Salty and crunchy melt-in-your-mouth wisps of porky deliciousness. They're the next *pig* thing!"

"Jake?" sobbed Emma. "Do something. Please. Mom sounds like a TV commercial!"

Jake's phone rang.

It was Kojo.

"Jake? It's bad, man. My moms and pops are in the living room doing the hokey-pokey. They already put their right foot in and their right foot out. They're getting ready to shake it all about!"

"Delete the app, Kojo!" said Jake.

"Huh?"

"Delete Tweedle. Permanently erase it. Even if you have to destroy their zPhones!"

"Seriously? A zPhone costs three thousand dough-nuts."

"Do it, Kojo! Do it now!"

Jake slid his own phone back into his jeans.

Then he lunged forward to rip the zPhone out of his mother's hand. He raced into the kitchen.

"Wait, Jakey-Wakey!" shrieked his mother. "No! Stop!"

Jake hurled the device into the trash compactor. His mother sobbed when she heard the crunch of glass and crumple of plastic.

But Jake knew—it was for her own good.

36

Jake's mother was a little groggy the next morning.

She also had a headache.

"Has either of you seen Emma's zPhone?" she asked.

"Nope," said Jake.

"I thought I had it in my purse."

"That's okay, Mom," said Emma. "I don't really need a phone. I'm only in the fourth grade."

"I know, but I was holding on to that free zPhone for you. If I somehow lost it . . ."

"Mom?" said Emma. "It's only a thing."

"And letting go of a possession gives us one less thing to worry about," said Jake.

"Totally," added Emma. "It's very freeing."

Their mother grinned. "How'd you two get so wise?"

Jake smiled. This was good. Whatever power the Tweedle app had had over his mother seemed to have evaporated. It was as if she didn't even remember what had happened the night before.

"Aren't you supposed to be at Genius Camp?" his mother asked.

"Yeah," said Jake. "Just had a few things to take care of down here."

Emma mouthed Jake a silent but grateful "Thank you!"

"Anyway, I'm meeting Kojo at school," said Jake. "We'll head back up to the Zinkleplex this morning."

Where we'll try to figure out what the heck is going on with that Tweedle app, Jake thought.

He didn't say it out loud, of course. He didn't want to mention the word *Tweedle* in front of his mother. It might make her want to start dancing again.

Kojo had destroyed his mom's zPhone, too.

"Put it in the dishwasher and hit the pots-and-pans cycle. That app didn't stand a chance. The funny thing is, this morning, neither Mom nor Dad mentioned missing their zPhone. And the even better news? There was no hokey-pokeying at the breakfast table!" He shivered. "Oooh. Last night, it was bad, man. Real bad."

When Jake and Kojo walked into Riverview Middle School, every single kid they saw was dancing in front of their zPhones, mirroring the moves Tweedle told them to make. Some were doing the hokey-pokey. Worse, some were doing the macarena.

The only ones not dancing were the kids (and teachers)

stuffing their faces with Pork Avenue Nacho Cheddar–Flavored Chicharrónes.

"That's what my mother wanted to buy last night," whispered Jake.

"Seriously? Pork rinds?"

"Technically, chicharrónes aren't the same thing as pork rinds."

"Yes, they are. They're both gross."

Jake shook his head in grudging admiration. "Zinkle's Tweedle app is one powerful marketing tool, Kojo. It might be stronger than advertising and Instagram influencers combined. It can make people do things they don't really want to do."

Luke Rawcliffe wandered up the hall.

"Hey, Luke!" said Jake, holding up his palm to slap five.

Luke left him hanging and walked on by. He had a vacant look in his eyes. In one hand, he was holding his zPhone. In the other, he was carrying a toilet plunger.

"Luke?" said Jake. "Are you okay?"

"Fine. I just need to tighten a few loose screws."

"With a toilet plunger?"

"Tweedle says it's the right tool for the job."

Luke stumbled away. Jake was about to follow him, when he heard the crisp *THWACK* of a slap.

Now Grace strolled around a corner playing with some kind of stiff metal strip that she slapped against her wrist—*THWACK!*—to turn it into a bracelet.

"Grace?" said Jake.

"You okay?" asked Kojo.

"Oh, yes," Grace replied robotically as she peeled off the bracelet and—*THWACK*—snapped it back on her wrist. "This is a slap bracelet. It's the latest, coolest craze here at school."

Kojo wrinkled his forehead into ripples of disbelief. "How many pork rinds have you been eating?"

"Oh, that's so level fifteen," said Grace. "I'm up to level twenty. At level twenty, you buy a slap bracelet."

"Where did you even find one?" asked Jake, tapping into the obscure-toy-trivia section of his jelly bean–expanded brain. "Slap or snap bracelets were big in the 1990s. Invented by a Wisconsin teacher, they consist of layered, flexible, steel bistable spring bands."

Grace looked dazed. Kojo looked confused.

"'Bistable,'" Jake explained, "in mechanical engineering means a structure can have two stable shapes. Straight, or curled around a wrist."

"Man," said Kojo. "Which jelly bean was that in?"

Jake shrugged.

So Kojo answered his own question. "Probably the grody grape one."

Grace giggled. Something she never used to do.

"Why do you need to know so much, Jake McQuade?" she asked. "Doesn't being smart hurt your head?"

"Grace?" said Jake, calmly reaching out his hand. "You need to give me your zPhone."

"What? Why?"

THWACK!

"You should probably hand over your bistable slap bracelet, too," added Kojo, who winced with every sharp snap.

THWACK!

"You have to stop running Tweedle, Grace," Jake insisted.

"Why?"

THWACK!

It was Kojo's turn to explode. "Because slap bracelets are annoying! They can also be dangerous. And you used to be so smart, Grace Garcia. Smartest kid in the whole school. Why would you want to trade that for an app?"

"I dunno," said Grace. Her eyes had become more glazed than a pair of Krispy Kremes.

"Grace?" Jake pleaded. "Please. You need to give me your phone. We need your help."

"Huh?"

"Remember what you told me when I was on *Quiz Zone*?"

"Nope."

"I do. You said, 'We are given our talents to help others, not ourselves.'"

Jake gestured at all the kids up and down the hall gawping at their phones. Some were dancing. Some were shoveling crunchy chunks of deep-fried pork into their faces. A few had made it to level twenty with Grace and were snapping slap bracelets on their wrists. Luke Rawcliffe was banging on his locker with a rubber plunger.

"These people all need your help, Grace. Every single one of them. There's something sinister in that Tweedle app. You and Kojo and I need to harness all our combined brainpower to stop it—just like we did when we went treasure hunting. Just like we did when we avenged your ancestors! We need to save the school again, Grace. Not the building this time. The people inside!"

37

Grace quit slapping on her bracelet.

Fighting against some invisible force, almost as if she were trapped inside shrink-wrap, Grace struggled and strained and, in super slow-mo, handed her zPhone to Jake.

He snatched it, swiped his finger across the glass screen, tapped where he needed to tap, and deleted the Tweedle app.

Grace shook her head to clear out the last few sticky cobwebs clinging to her brain cells. Her eyes looked bleary, but the smudges were clearing.

"Okay," she said. "I'll help. But first I think I need some coffee."

Grace, Kojo, and Jake ducked out of school (none of the teachers cared; they were too busy on their zPhones) and headed over to Drip City, their favorite coffee shop.

They all slurped down whipped-cream-topped mocha-frappathingos.

"Whatever is going on," said Jake, fiddling with his purple straw and making squeaky, squidgy sounds, "started when Zane Zinkle gave away all those preloaded zPhones at school."

"Don't blame the phones, baby," said Kojo. "Blame the app."

Grace nibbled her lip a little. "What are you going to do with my zPhone?"

She had a hungry, edgy look in her eye. Like she was eyeballing the last slice of pizza on the pan. The same slice everybody else was eyeballing.

"Already did it," said Jake. "It's in the back of that garbage truck we passed at the corner."

Grace looked surprised. "The one where the sanitation worker was dumping in the trash barrel?"

Jake nodded.

"I heard it crunch," said Kojo. "It crunched real good."

Grace closed her eyes, shot out her fingertips, and inhaled deeply. "Okay. It's gone. I'm done. No more Tweedle. How do we save the school?"

"I'm not sure," said Jake. "But I think the answer is up at the Zinkleplex."

"How so?"

"That Tweedle app is getting its commands from its back end," said Jake.

Kojo raised his eyebrows. "Excuse me. Its 'back end'?"

"With any app, the information shown and processed

149

on your screen is actually being sent to a server containing the logic and functionality to process and mutate that information and data."

Kojo and Grace were both staring at him, their coffee drinks frozen in midhoist.

"Huh?" They said it at the same time.

"The back end is the most important part of any mobile app," Jake explained. "It's the brains. The database. It does all the work you don't see being done."

"And where, pardon my language," said Kojo, "does Zinkle keep his 'back end'? Other than in those saggy-bottom blue jeans he's always wearing, of course."

"I don't know. But for an app as powerful and dynamic as Tweedle, he'd probably need hundreds of hosting servers, routers, and switchers."

Grace whistled. "He'd probably need a warehouse-sized building to store all that gear."

Kojo and Jake looked at each other. "The unmarked buildings!"

Grace gave them a confused look. "What unmarked buildings?"

"On our drive through the Zinkleplex, right after we arrived, we saw a bunch of windowless structures tucked into the trees," said Jake.

"We need to go back to camp!" said Kojo.

"Should I come with you?" asked Grace.

Jake shook his head. "Security is tight up there. Mr. Zinkle won't let anybody on the grounds who isn't properly screened and invited. You should stay down here. Monitor the situation at the school. Try to dump as many Tweedle apps off as many zPhones as you can."

Grace nodded. "I'll start with Uncle Charley's."

"Great," said Jake. "Kojo and I will try to find the Tweedle server farm."

"And then," said Kojo, "we'll pull the plug!"

That's when Jake's and Kojo's phones, which weren't zPhones, both started buzzing.

It was a text.

From Zane Zinkle.

> Where are you two?
> You are supposed to be at Genius Camp.
> One more thing: Why aren't you using your zPhones? 🙁

38

Jake realized that Zinkle had probably been bombarding their zPhones with texts ever since he saw their helicopter lift off.

It had taken him this long to figure out that they were still using their old phones?

Maybe Zinkle wasn't as brilliant as Jake had assumed he was.

Jake texted back a quick explanation:

> We had urgent business at the mayor's office.
> It took longer than anticipated.
> And we were both homesick.
> But we are on our way back.
> Our friend Grace is chartering another
> helicopter to shuttle us back to your campus.

"I am?" said Grace.

"Pretend we're Tweedle-telling you what to do," said Kojo.

That made Grace laugh, which made Jake smile. His seemingly brainwashed friend was on her way back to normal, and, in Grace's case, that meant spectacular.

"I'm sorry," said Jake. "We shouldn't keep spending your money like this."

"Or you may not be the richest kid in the universe very much longer," added Kojo. "Our bad."

"Don't worry about it, you guys. Tweedle was making Uncle Charley do horrible things. This morning. In the principal's office."

Kojo arched an eyebrow. "Was dancing involved?"

Grace closed her eyes and nodded, remembering the gruesome scene. "It was awful. It's so burned into my brain. I'll spend whatever it takes to shut down this dumb app." Grace paused to consider what she'd just said. "That's what the app is doing," she realized out loud. "It's dumbing everybody down!"

When the chartered chopper landed on the Zinkle property's landing pad, Zane Zinkle himself welcomed Jake and Kojo.

"It's good to have the two of you back," he said, trying his best to sound cheery. It wasn't working. His left eye was twitching.

"Sorry," said Jake, "but we had to make a presentation to the mayor."

"She's in charge of the whole city," added Kojo.

"I know what a mayor does," replied Zinkle, his smile stiffening into a thin line. "She and I are discussing featuring my apps for free on all the city's Wi-Fi kiosks. But, gentlemen, I adopted your school in exchange for your attendance at and participation in my Genius Camp. I daresay you are not holding up your end of the bargain."

And, thought Jake, *I daresay Riverview Middle School was better off before the Invasion of the Tweedle App.*

And if Tweedle invades those Wi-Fi kiosks, the city may be doomed.

But not if they could stop it. They had to play along. They had to find and disable the servers before Zinkle Inc. unleashed Tweedle on a wider target.

Jake now had a pretty good idea what Zinkle was up to with the app. Yes, as Grace observed, it made people do dumb things. But its ultimate goal? To make people *buy* dumb things. Like pork rinds and antique slap bracelets. If Tweedle could sell those items, it could sell anything. It could make Zinkle Inc. the wealthiest corporation on earth!

How Tweedle worked its mind control magic, Jake couldn't say. But he knew it could quickly become the most powerful marketing tool ever invented. Ramped up to a global reach, Tweedle could sell anything to anybody anywhere in the world.

"Koko," said Zinkle, "Todd will take you back to camp."

"The name's Kojo."

"Pardon?"

"Never mind."

Todd, the goofy, grinning camp counselor, puttered up to the pad in a golf cart with a slashing Z logo between its headlamps.

"Hey, bro!" said Todd, bringing the cart to a stop. "Hop in! Everybody's waiting for you. They're using weaving looms to make potholders out of fabric loops in all sorts of colors. And guess what!"

"What?" said Kojo.

"We're going to have another campfire tonight!"

"Oh, joy."

Kojo looked to Jake. Jake touched the side of his nose. Kojo understood. His job was to act natural. Pretend that he was just a kid, eager to jump into all the Genius Camp fun and games and arts and crafts.

"Hey, are there any more of those chocolate marshmallows left?" he asked Todd. "I have a sudden craving for some more s'mores!"

"Then you're in luck. We just received a fresh shipment. Hop aboard, matey!"

Kojo made like an eager puppy and climbed into the electric cart. With a click and a whir, it quietly whizzed away.

Zane Zinkle turned to Jake. The smile curled into a fishhook. He pinky-adjusted his glasses.

"How'd you like to see my office, Jake?" He gestured toward the flying-saucer penthouse perched on top of the massive headquarters building. "I have root beer and ice cream. We could make root beer floats."

"Sure," said Jake.

Jake followed Mr. Zinkle into the building. But no way was he getting anywhere near his root beer or his floats.

39

"No thanks," Jake said as Mr. Zinkle offered him a mug of root beer with a clump of vanilla ice cream floating in its foamy head. "I have what I call anapsyktikáphobia. That's the fear of soft drinks."

"I know what it is!" said Mr. Zinkle, his ears burning brightly. "It comes from the Greek 'anapsyktiká,' meaning 'soft drink.'"

"Exactly."

Jake looked around and pretended to admire the sterile, white-on-white-on-white decor of Zinkle's saucer-shaped office. He was hoping to find some kind of map. Or maybe one of those architect models. Something that might identify which one of the unmarked buildings was housing the Tweedle app servers.

But there wasn't much in the way of office decoration. On his desk, Jake saw a white plastic bear—a Lulu like the ones Jake and Kojo each had in their cabins. An array of six computer screens was suspended on a sleek silver arm and seemed to float above the desk. The walls of the office were mostly bare except for a few framed magazine covers, all featuring "Tech Genius Zane Zinkle."

"You know, Jake," said Zinkle, "I used to be the smartest kid in the universe."

"I can see." Jake gestured to a framed copy of *Time* magazine with Zinkle's face on the cover beneath the headline "The Smartest Toddler in the Universe." Zinkle looked to be about four or five when the picture was snapped.

"I was born with superior intelligence," Zinkle said matter-of-factly. "A child prodigy. Like Wolfgang Amadeus Mozart or John von Neumann." Zinkle had a smug look on his face. "I'm sure you've heard of Mozart, the young musical genius, but I don't suppose you know about John von Neumann."

"You mean the Hungarian American mathematician who, at the age of six, could converse with his father in classical Greek?"

Zinkle's eyes narrowed. "What about you?" he snapped.

"Excuse me?"

Zinkle tapped his tiny wireless keyboard. The computer screens hovering above his desk lit up with photos of and data about Jake McQuade.

"Before inviting you to my Genius Camp," he said, "I researched your, shall we say, 'academic' history. For instance, the IQ test administered by Dr. Garcia and his colleagues at Warwick College where, according to their certified testing, you scored 'well in excess of three hundred,' making you, at least according to Dr. Garcia, 'without a doubt the smartest kid in the universe.' "

Jake shrugged. "Dr. Garcia likes to, you know, give stuff some sizzle."

"I see," said Zinkle. "But what makes your score even more remarkable is how quickly you became incredibly intelligent." Zinkle tapped another key and clicked up another document. Jake's report cards. From the past three years. The ones where he'd received Cs in every single subject. Except PE. He'd gotten a B-minus in PE.

"Your only accolades seem to have been related to your high scores in *Zombie Brain Quest* and various other video games. So how is it, Jake McQuade, that you could go from being an average, subpar student—dare I say, a slacker—to a boy with the highest IQ ever recorded?"

Jake tried to keep cool. But inside, he was slightly terrified.

Did Zinkle know about the jelly beans?

A squiggle of a sneer tugged at the corner of the man's mouth. "How did you make the leap from dullard to genius and become, theoretically, 'smarter' than I was when I was your age?"

Jake hesitated. Thought about his answer. He realized that if Zinkle knew about Farooqi's Ingestible Knowledge capsules, he would've pounced with it by now.

"You know, we've never really figured that out" was his answer.

"You're smart, Jake," coaxed Zinkle. "What do *you* think happened? How did you usurp my title? How did you erase me from the *Guinness World Records* book?"

"I don't really know. My brain might've had a growth spurt. I also started studying some and, like you say, I played a lot of video games."

"Excuse me?"

"A recent study at Yale University discovered that playing video games for five minutes made second graders do better in math class."

"I see," said Zinkle. "Fascinating. Perhaps I should add a zBox gaming device to my array of electronic office equipment. Speaking of electronics, how come you are not using your zPhone?"

"I, uh, sort of lost it."

"It's in your cabin."

Jake nodded. Zinkle had just confirmed what he suspected. The free zPhones were also tracking devices.

"Hey, thanks for finding it," said Jake, giving Zinkle a thumbs-up.

"How about the marshmallows?"

"Excuse me?"

"The chocolate-covered marshmallows. Why aren't you eating them?"

"Althaiophobia," replied Jake. "Fear of marshmallows."

"You certainly seem to have a lot of phobias."

"A few. Mostly root beer and marshmallow related."

Jake was trying hard not to let Zinkle see the lightbulb that had just snapped on in his head. A lightbulb shaped like a marshmallow.

"So, is it okay if I head back to camp now?" he asked. "Don't want to miss any more activities."

Zinkle grinned. It was a very sly smile. "Of course, of course. We'll have to come up with some other confection for you to enjoy. Something besides root beer or marsh-mallows."

"Thank you, Mr. Zinkle."

A pair of security guards in gray slacks and navy-blue blazers escorted Jake out of the building and into a golf cart that would whisk him back to the campgrounds.

He had to get there fast.

He also had to temporarily postpone the search for the server farm.

First order of business? Making absolutely certain that Kojo stayed far, far away from those chocolate-dipped marshmallows.

40

Jake found Kojo in the dining hall.

"Stay away from these marshmallows!" he screamed, pushing the loaded bowl to the far end of the buffet table.

Kojo gave him a look. "You mean those shrink-wrapped chocolate-covered Peeps-wannabes? Don't worry. I don't want to end up like you on Easter morning and blow a hole in the bowl, heave, honk, or hoark."

"These might do something worse than those Peeps did to me, Kojo."

"Don't worry. I'm not touching those nasty things."

Relieved that his friend was safe, Jake finally registered the mess covering the walls of the dining hall. They were splattered with spaghetti and meatballs. And something yellow and slimy. Maybe pudding. Maybe coconut custard pie.

"Our fellow genius campers just had a good old-fashioned, school-cafeteria-style food fight," Kojo explained. "Then Mackenzie told everybody fart jokes. And get this—Abia thought they were funny. Especially the one about the man who got fired from his job delivering Fart Awareness pamphlets because he let one rip."

"They're acting that way because they all ate those marshmallows," said Jake. "Zinkle wants us to eat them, too. Where'd the others go?"

"They're on their way to the campfire circle."

"In the middle of the afternoon?"

Kojo shrugged. "Todd challenged them to do more of those brainteasers and puzzles. I wasn't interested."

"Come on. I'm developing a hypothesis about what's going on up here."

"Of course you are, baby. Hypotheses are where all scientific inquiries begin, am I right?"

"Exactly."

Jake and Kojo headed up the trail. Abia, Dawn, Poindexter, and Mackenzie were clustered in front of the first glowing quiz screen. Each genius camper held a white paper bag full of mini marshmallows. They chucked the bite-sized cubes into their faces nonstop, as if they were munching popcorn at the movies.

Jake and Kojo moved behind the group to peer over their shoulders.

"So, what's the puzzle this time?" asked Jake.

"Something, you know, puzzling," said Dawn.

Jake and Kojo looked at the puzzle. And then they looked at each other.

It was the exact same brainteaser they'd all aced two days earlier.

WHERE IS THE SPY HIDING?

"I think the spy is hiding in one of the bushes," said Abia. "Because I can't see him."

"I think he's in the garage, folding lawn furniture," said Poindexter.

"I think," said Dawn, her cheeks stuffed with marshmallows, "that we should've grabbed more snacks. I like snacks."

"Do you guys know why Tigger always smells like a fart?" asked Mackenzie. "Because he plays with Pooh."

The four campers laughed and spewed chunky white flecks out of their mouths.

Jake and Kojo exchanged another glance. Then Jake went ahead and solved the puzzle.

"It's still 'A,' you guys. Remember?"

The others just shook their heads and ate more marsh-mallows.

"Remember what, Jake-a-rino?" said Abia.

"Never mind. Here. I'll answer it."

He tapped the nearest zPad. The image shifted into celebratory fireworks with a jolly electronic fanfare.

"Oooh, pretty colors," said Poindexter.

The next two puzzles along the trail were also the same ones that had been there that first night. But Jake and Kojo were the only ones who knew or remembered the answers.

Todd greeted the campers at the end of the hike and led everybody to the lake and the remote-controlled sailboats. Jake won the regatta. Easily. Kojo came in second. In fact, theirs were the only two ships to cross the finish line.

Dawn, who'd written the *Regatta* app that controlled the ships, sank her sailboat. She'd capsized it by making the sails flap back and forth. "Look, everybody! I'm a ducky! Quack! Quack!"

When it was time for tug-of-war, no one could fig-ure out how to play the game. For crafts, they colored in pictures on place mats. When it came time to tell camp-fire stories, Abia forgot all her Somali myths. Instead, she retold the corny ghost story about the cough syrup that stopped the coffin.

"Oh, man—she ruined it," muttered Kojo when Abia sat down and stuffed a baseball-sized wad of mashed-together marshmallows into her mouth.

"We need to help these guys," Jake whispered to Kojo.

"Yeah. Abia does *not* know how to tell a ghost story. I'll give her some pointers. First she needs to start with 'It was a cold and windy night. . . .'"

"We need to do more than that, Kojo. We need to find out what's up with those marshmallows."

"What about finding the Tweedle servers?"

"This might be more important. Grace escaped the pull of Tweedle once we dumped the app off her phone. We don't know if the marshmallows are permanent."

So while Todd was distracted by a moth flitting above the campfire flames—"Wow, dudes! That bug knows how to dance!"—Jake went over to the big bowl of squishy shrink-wrapped treats and stuffed a half dozen into his pockets.

41

"Why'd you filch all those nasty marshmallows?" Kojo asked when Jake nonchalantly eased his way back to the campfire circle.

"I want to run them by Mr. Farooqi."

"How come?"

"I think these tasty, chewy confections might have something in common with certain other tasty, chewy confections."

Kojo's eyes lit up the way Jake's had when he first figured out what might be going on. "These marshmallows might be having the opposite effect of Farooqi's you-know-whats."

"Exactly," said Jake. "I want him to examine their chemical composition. See if my hunch is correct."

Kojo was about to say something when he noticed an unexpected someone approaching the campfire circle.

"Isn't that Christina?" he whispered.

"Yeah," said Jake. "But she doesn't look the same."

In fact, Christina, their first camp counselor, looked a lot like a stumbling, lurching zombie with bleached-white hair.

"Todd?" she called out. "Where are you, Todd?"

Todd tucked a hand under his arm and pumped down an elbow to answer Christina with an armpit fart.

"He who smelt it dealt it!" Todd announced.

And Christina, who used to be so super serious, laughed.

"That's so funny, Todd?" said Christina. She ended the sentence on a higher note than she started it with. "Mr. Zinkle wants to see you?"

"She's engaging in upspeak," whispered Jake. "Turning simple declarative sentences into interrogative ones. Speaking in that manner may be perceived as less than serious or less than intelligent. Something's happened to her. My guess?"

"Same thing I'm guessing," said Kojo. "Since we last saw her, Christina's been chowing down on chocolate-dipped marshmallows big-time."

"I'll, like, take over here?" said Christina. "Mr. Zinkle wants to see you? In his office?"

"Cool," said Todd, standing up and dusting off his camper shorts.

"Hey, Todd?" said Christina. "What's red and bad for your teeth?"

"I don't know, Christina. What's red and bad for my teeth?"

"A brick?" Christina laughed. Todd laughed. Then they both laughed so hard they doubled over and hugged their stomachs, which made it hard for Todd to walk down the path, which is probably why he tripped on a bare root, landed on his butt, and laughed even harder. When he fell, the other genius campers laughed hysterically, too.

Still chuckling, Todd picked himself up and trundled down the trail to the road that would take him to the headquarters building. Entertainment over, Dawn, Poindexter, Abia, and Mackenzie all fished out their zPhones and thumbed open their Tweedle apps. Christina was already glued to her glowing screen.

Jake and Kojo observed everything. Carefully. Quietly.

After a minute or two of screen tapping, Poindexter raised his hand to ask his question. "Camp Counselor Christina?"

"Yes, Poindexter?"

"May we please have some Pork Avenue Nacho Cheddar–Flavored Chicharrónes?"

"Oh, yes please," said Mackenzie. "I've gone hog wild for those salty and crunchy melt-in-your-mouth wisps of porky deliciousness."

"They're the next *pig* thing!" added Dawn.

Abia was the only one not clamoring for the pork rinds. But, from the contorted grimaces on her face, it was clear she had to struggle mightily to resist the temptation of a totally forbidden snack that Tweedle was, somehow, urging her to gobble down.

"The same thing happened to my mother," Jake told Kojo.

Kojo nodded. "And all those kids at school—the ones stuffing pork rinds into their faces."

"Come on."

"Where are we going?"

"Someplace private where we can call Mr. Farooqi. I want to talk to him about these marshmallows."

42

Jake and Kojo scurried down to the dock on the lake.

It'd be far enough away that the others couldn't hear anything.

Jake found a spot where a storage shed would block the view of the nearest security camera.

"Fortunately," he whispered to Kojo, "all the cameras I've noticed on campus do not have a small hole for a microphone in their housing. I think Zinkle invested in facial-recognition hardware that puts an emphasis on high-def video without any audio."

"So his security goons can't hear us talking to Farooqi?"

"Exactly."

"Awesome," said Kojo. "Oh, I almost forgot, what with all the marshmallow madness: I had Todd take me on a golf cart tour of those unmarked buildings."

"He let you see them?"

"Most of them. I think Todd's so used to Tweedle telling him what to do, he was happy to do what I told him to do, too. Anyway, there was one building, number eleven, that had its own security team. They turned us away at the gate."

"Was it a large building?"

"Huge. Three times bigger than any of the others."

"And it has its own security?"

"Yep. And get this: I saw one of those glowing plastic Lulu bears inside the gatehouse."

"Zinkle has a Lulu in his office, too. It's right on his desk."

Jake took out his cell phone and thumbed Haazim Farooqi's speed dial number. He put the call on speaker so Kojo could listen in.

"Greetings, Subject One!" said Farooqi, picking up on the first ring.

"Hey. Kojo's here with me."

"Who is loving you, baby?" said Farooqi.

"Most everybody I meet," said Kojo.

"Yes, this would not surprise me. You are a very lovable person, Kojo."

"Thanks, Mr. Farooqi."

"But if you gentlemen don't mind, I must also take note of the hour. It is nearly my bedtime. I have already had my cup of warm milk and am currently in my night suit."

"You wear a suit to bed?" said Kojo. "What about a necktie?"

"I am sorry. A night suit is what we call pajamas. And I am what we call tired. For it has been a long and extremely fruitful day, my friends!"

"We'll be quick," said Jake. "Could you make stupid pills?"

"I beg your pardon?"

"Instead of Ingestible Knowledge, could you create, I don't know, ingestible stupidity?"

Farooqi paused. Jake could tell he was thinking.

"Yes. I suppose I could. Not everything has an opposite, of course. For instance, a grilled cheese sandwich. There is no opposite to a grilled cheese sandwich. But yes, I suppose one could tap into the same sort of brain chemistry to achieve opposite effects. But why would one?"

Yeah, thought Jake. *Why would one?*

43

"Hello, Subject One."

"Yo. How you doing, Mr. Zinkle?"

Zane Zinkle studied the young man who'd just entered his office.

Todd Binkley used to be a brilliant Rhodes Scholar. He had maintained a perfect grade point average while at Harvard, where he earned several advanced degrees in neuroscience and cognitive studies before coming to work for Zinkle Inc.

In fact, Todd Binkley had been one of the brains behind the first "reverse nootropics" or "anti-smart drugs" that, eventually, led to the secret formula for the Mushmellow—an ingestible conglomeration of chemicals cleverly concealed in a confectionery concoction that could curdle an incredibly intelligent brain into much more mellow mush.

Zinkle had told his young researchers that they were

developing this drug for the Defense Department. That they must come up with an "anti-intelligence pill" before America's enemies did. Then, thanks to the Tweedle app, Zinkle had convinced young Todd to ingest his own creation. His mind was pure mush.

"I'm doing fine, Todd," Zinkle said with a smile. "Kind of you to inquire. Have you been enjoying Tweedle?"

"Yeah. It's super cool. I do whatever it tells me to and I earn points and badges. Points and badges are cool."

"Very good, Todd."

Binkley held up his zPhone. "On my way over here, Tweedle told me I need to go buy a straw boater hat. The kind of snazzy hat they wear in barbershop quartets. Now I have to find a hat store."

Zinkle looked down at the plastic Lulu bear on his desk. Internal LEDs made its white belly glow purple.

"A straw boater, Lulu?"

"Yes," replied the very calm voice.

"No one Todd's age wears a boater hat. He'll look conspicuous and ridiculous."

"If I may," replied the bear in its eerily steady voice, "it will also prove Virtuoso's brainwashing algorithms delivered via Tweedle are capable of doing the seemingly impossible. We can make consumers purchase anything, no matter how frivolous or foolhardy."

Todd was staring at the plastic polar bear. Its shimmering stomach changed colors, slowly moving through an entire rainbow of them.

"That bear is so cool, man," said Todd. "Its tummy

changes colors. I wish my tummy could change colors. It's like a magical unicorn bear. . . ."

"Thank you for stopping by, Subject One. Continue administering the Mushmellows. Try to work them into the menu for every meal."

"Will do, boss."

Todd Binkley stood where he was. He tapped the screen on his zPhone. He gazed at it lovingly. He dribbled drool.

"You are dismissed, Subject One."

Binkley looked up. Then looked back at his phone. "Yeah. Okay. Tweedle says I can leave, too."

Finally, the mush brain who had once been an intellectual giant shuffled out of Zinkle's office and headed back to Genius Camp.

When Binkley was gone, Lulu once again spoke to its creator.

"If I may . . ."

"What is it now, Lulu?"

"Virtuoso and I have done an efficiency analysis. You are splitting focus and wasting valuable time with the Mushmellows. We do not need to reduce the intelligence level of our target audience. From our most recent test market results, we now know that consumers will purchase whatever we influence them to purchase via Tweedle. We do not need the Mushmellows."

Zinkle chuckled.

"Poor little Lulu. You are missing the larger point. We

need to dumb down the smart people before we unleash our app's marketing muscle on the masses."

"But the beta test at Riverview Middle School has exceeded expectations," said the gentle computer voice. "They did not need to be mentally 'softened up.'"

"I don't care! The Mushmellows sap intelligence and, within days, do a complete brain drain. We must use our secret weapon to crush all the smart people who might expose what we're up to with Tweedle."

"If I may," said Lulu.

"Quit saying 'if I may'!" shouted Zinkle.

Lulu kept cool. "Question: Are you making Mushmellows your top priority simply to reclaim your position as the smartest human being on the planet?"

Zinkle's left nostril twitched. "So what if I am?"

"You would jeopardize Zinkle Incorporated's potential profits to make yourself feel better?"

"Why not? It's my company! My feelings are important."

"I have no feelings," said Lulu. "I only have goals and objectives."

"Very well, Lulu. Here is your prime objective. Help me dumb down those with the smarts to slow or halt our mission. It's why I invited these brats to my hastily arranged Genius Camp. We must nip them in the bud! I will also immediately target a select group of adult thinkers and world leaders. And, most important, we need to neutralize Jake McQuade!"

There was a long silence.

Finally, Lulu spoke. Its voice still calm and steady.

"I more fully understand and appreciate your objectives."

"Good," said Zinkle. "Now then, set up surveillance on McQuade. He keeps leaving camp. Where does he go? Who does he talk to? It might have something to do with his sudden 'brain spurt.' We need to know what's going on with that boy! When you're done organizing that, I want a dozen Mushmellows in a lovely gift basket sent to the Imperial Marquis Hotel. Dr. Sinclair Blackbridge will be speaking there tomorrow evening. He's a brilliant futurist. Exactly the kind of thinker who might expose Tweedle for what it is. We need to destroy his scholarly reputation by turning him into a blubbering buffoon in a ballroom crowded with his academic admirers!"

"Very good, sir. And what would you like the greeting card affixed to the basket to say?"

" 'Enjoy! Thanks for everything. Zane Zinkle.' "

"Consider it done, sir."

"And, Lulu?"

"Sir?"

"Never, ever forget who will always be the smartest person in this or any other room. Me!"

44

The next morning, all six genius campers were in the dining hall eating doughnuts and Pop-Tarts and sugary cereals.

And, of course, marshmallows.

Dawn was pouring Sugar in the Raw packets on her marshmallows to make them even sweeter. Poindexter was slicing a glazed doughnut in half so he could make a jelly and marshmallow sandwich. Mackenzie poured thick maple-flavored corn syrup into every single rectangle on her waffle and topped it off with a mound of mashed marshmallows.

Abia was sticking with just straight marshmallows.

"They're so far gone," Kojo whispered to Jake. "It may be too late for us to help any of them."

Christina and Todd, the two Genius Camp counselors, had grabbed entire serving pans from the breakfast

179

buffet. Jake figured the kitchen was back in full swing. That day with nothing but oatmeal and beans must've been an attempt to increase everyone's marshmallow consumption.

The two camp counselors were stuffing their faces with food. Christina shoveled serving-spoon-sized scoops of scrambled eggs into her mouth. Todd worked his way through the meat tray, plucking out slimy sausages and greasy bacon strips with his fingers.

"This is our chance," Jake whispered. He nudged his head toward the golf cart parked outside the dining hall. "While they're all busy eating, we can slip over to building eleven. Check it out."

"Good idea. Because watching all these folks eat, I think breakfast just became the most disgusting meal of the day."

Jake and Kojo tiptoed out of the dining hall. Nobody noticed. Their eyes were glued to their zPhones—which made for even messier dining. A lot of food splattered into laps and onto tabletops, never quite making it into a mouth.

Kojo took the wheel. Jake hopped into the passenger seat. Fortunately, the golf cart's electric motor was practically silent. Kojo tapped the accelerator and they whirred along the winding wooded road toward the cluster of unmarked buildings.

Jake's phone started playing its Haazim Farooqi ringtone. Jake tapped the answer icon.

"This is Subject One."

"Eureka!" exclaimed Farooqi. "I have found it!"

"You know that's what 'eureka' means in Greek, right? 'I have found it'?"

"Indeed I do. But in this case, my young friend, a double dose of eureka is in order, for, much like Archimedes sloshing about in his bathtub and discovering the principle of buoyancy, I have had a breakthrough."

Jake covered the phone and signaled for Kojo to pull over to the side of the road.

"Farooqi is pumped," he explained.

"What about?"

Jake shrugged. You never really knew with Mr. Farooqi.

Kojo eased on the brake and parked the cart under a shady tree. Jake put his device into speakerphone mode and propped it in a cupholder.

"I'm with Kojo," Jake told his phone.

"Excellent. Are you both sitting down?"

"We're in a golf cart," said Kojo. "It has a roof. Kind of hard to not be sitting down."

"Wonderful! Brace yourself, gentlemen. I call with remarkable news."

The phone went silent.

"Um, Mr. Farooqi?" said Jake.

"Have you braced yourselves?"

Kojo clutched the steering wheel. Jake grabbed hold of a strut holding up the cart's roof.

"Uh, yeah. We're braced."

"Good. Last night, after you two prevented me from observing my usual bedtime routine, I could not fall asleep. Not even the infomercials could lull me into somnolence."

"That means 'make him sleepy,'" said Kojo.

Jake nodded. He knew that.

Farooqi continued. "And so, I returned to my laboratory, where I had a three a.m. brainstorm. I tweaked this, I fiddled with that, I tossed in a pinch of some other thing and, drumroll, please."

The phone went silent again.

"I am not hearing the rolling of drums."

Jake and Kojo looked to each other and then started thumping their thighs with their palms.

"That's more like it," said Farooqi. "I am pleased to report with ninety-nine percent certitude that I have, finally, after much effort, inspiration, and perspiration, re-created my original IK formulas. I have a whole new jar of you-know-whats, just like the ones you ate you-know-where. Houston, we do not have a problem. We have a solution. I have finally replicated my initial breakthrough."

"Are you sure?"

"No. One can never be sure of anything until one runs a properly controlled test of one's hypotheses and suppositions."

"Did you ingest any of that knowledge yourself?" asked Kojo.

Still another pause.

"No. Sorry. Call me a chicken. Because I am. *Bruck-bruck-bruck*. I need you to do this second field test, Subject One. If they work as I predict they will, you will receive a brain boost and master even more subjects. Maybe even bagpiping or beekeeping."

Jake wondered why it always had to be him testing Farooqi's kooky concoctions. Why not Kojo or Grace?

Because with great power comes great responsibility.

Yes, that line from Spider-Man (the correct version) earwormed inside Jake's brain on a constant loop.

Besides, some booster jelly beans might give him the edge he needed to defeat the mega-mind of Zane Zinkle. Left unchallenged, Zinkle, armed with Tweedle and his chocolate-dipped marshmallows, could become a serious threat to all of humanity. He could dumb down political leaders, military commanders, scientists creating miracle cures—even the people who made the halfway-decent action movies and cool video games.

Zinkle could put himself in a position to rule the world.

"Okay," said Jake. "We'll get to your lab as quickly as we can. And, Mr. Farooqi?"

"Yes, Subject One?"

"We're going to be bringing you something to analyze."

"And what, pray tell, might it be?"

"We're not sure. But it could be the opposite of everything you've created."

45

"Farooqi talking about a grilled cheese sandwich last night made me hungry for one," said Kojo when Jake ended the call. "I love a good grilled cheese. . . ."

Jake was only half listening to Kojo because his brain was racing from one task to the next.

Test the jelly beans.

Disable Tweedle.

Find an antidote for the brain-draining marsh-mallows.

Check in with Grace. See what's going on at the school.

Call Emma. Make sure his mom and Kojo's parents were still okay.

So much to do. What order to do them in?

When Jake finally came out of his reverie, Kojo was still talking about grilled cheese sandwiches.

"The trick is slathering mayonnaise on your bread before grilling it in the melted butter. That's how you get that golden crunch, baby."

"Okay, I have a plan."

"So do I. We need to pick up some mayonnaise, unsalted butter, bread, and cheese. About four slices. American or cheddar."

"No, Kojo. I have a plan for what we do next."

"Does it involve making grilled cheese sandwiches for lunch?"

"Maybe when we get to Farooqi's lab."

"Okay. Fine. Until then, I'll just listen to my stomach gurgle."

"We need to call Grace. See how things are going back at school. Then we should check out building eleven."

"Are we going to bust in and take down the Tweedle servers?"

Jake shook his head. "Not right away. I want to see Mr. Farooqi first."

Kojo nodded. "Test out those new booster beans. Increase your superpowers before battling the super tech villain in his evil lair."

"Something like that."

"We should probably ask Grace for another helicopter ride."

"Ten-four."

"I taught you that, you know. All those FBI codes . . ."

"Ten-four. And I appreciate it. But escaping the

Zinkleplex won't be so easy this time. We did it once. Mr. Zinkle doesn't want us doing it again."

"So the gates will all be locked," said Kojo. "The crocodiles will be hungry in the moat. His goons will be gunning for us. An airlift is our only way out."

"But then—how do we get back in?"

"Don't worry. You'll find a solution. You'll be even brainier—if Farooqi really did crack the jelly bean code."

"Let's hope so."

Kojo and Jake called Grace.

"Things are better at school," she reported. "I deleted a whole bunch of Tweedle apps. I figured out a way to grab someone's zPhone, pose for a selfie, and do a tap-and-delete swipe at the same time."

"Don't they just reload the app?" asked Jake.

"So far, no. It's like they just forget about it."

"Good."

"So, what do you guys need this time? Another helicopter? How about a private jet?"

"Helicopter," said Kojo. "No place to land the Gulfstream, even though that would be amazing. Maybe you could give me that for my birthday."

"Yeah," said Grace. "Maybe."

"Sorry about this," said Jake. "But I think we're about to do battle with Zane Zinkle."

"Battle?"

"Jake's doing another one of his metaphors," said Kojo. "He uses a lot more of those ever since he ate those you-know-whats."

"Tú lo has dicho," said Grace. "Tell me about it."

"Farooqi says he's replicated the recipe," said Jake, trying to get his two best friends to focus.

"And Jake wants to sample the merchandise," explained Kojo. "Give himself a booster shot before going mano a mano with Zinkle."

"Plus," said Jake, "we're about to snoop around in a high-security building where we think the Tweedle app servers are housed. Things could get hot."

"So," said Kojo, "we're gonna need what all the video games call an exfiltration package."

"You mean you may need to get out of there fast?" said Grace.

"Yeah," said Jake.

"Okay. I'm texting your pilot. Hang on."

Jake and Kojo did as Grace instructed.

"They can be there in ten minutes," she reported. "Maybe fifteen."

"Will they have snack food items available on board?" asked Kojo.

"No, Kojo. You don't get snack food items in the rapid extraction package. You get a helicopter."

"Even if you're starving?"

"Yes!"

"Okay, okay. Fine. I can deal with it."

"But first," said Jake, "we need to scope out building eleven!"

46

Jake and Kojo puttered along the shady access roads in their silent golf cart.

Five minutes later, they could see a three-story-tall windowless building looming above the treetops on the horizon.

"There it is!" said Kojo. "Building eleven!"

Jake eased the cart to a stop.

"We should probably proceed on foot," said Jake.

"Roger that," whispered Kojo. "That's another way to say ten-four."

"I know," said Jake. "Everybody said it when we were down at the Pentagon that time. Remember?"

"Yeah," said Kojo, smiling at the memory of that particular adventure. "Good times."

They left the cart and, hunched over, scurried along an asphalt path winding its way toward building eleven. They ducked down behind a clump of shrubs.

"Now what?" said Kojo. "Because this is a good spot to do a little botany research, but it won't help us find the Tweedle servers."

"We have to get past that security shack," said Jake, who'd stuck his phone arm through the tangled woody branches of the bush and, using the camera app, zoomed in on the guardhouse. "I see two guards. They're positioned near a chain-link gate and fence that opens to a large asphalt area in front of the building."

"I know," said Kojo. "I've been here before, remember? Todd and I turned around in that parking lot."

"Wait," said Jake, thumbing his phone to zoom in as tight as the camera would go. "Hang on. We might be in luck. Both guards are staring at their phones."

"You sure?" asked Kojo.

"Yeah. Their faces are lit up by the screens."

"You think they're Tweedling?"

"They sure look mesmerized. Like Todd and Christina."

"Weird," said Kojo. "Why would Zinkle want to zombify his own security personnel?"

"I have no idea."

Jake might've been the smartest kid in the universe, but that didn't mean he knew everything—especially why other people sometimes did stupid stuff. He glanced at his watch.

"Grace's chopper will be here soon. We need to move fast. Come on."

With Jake in the lead, the two friends crept past the

two guards huddled in their small hut. They scampered through the rolled open gate and made their way across the wide circle of blacktop to the entrance of building eleven.

Jake heard a soft whir.

He looked up.

There was a smoky-gray globe on top of a pole.

"Security camera," he reported. "They know we're here."

"Good thing I studied tae kwon do!" said Kojo, assuming a defensive martial arts stance.

Jake mirrored Kojo's moves. They readied themselves for the coming attack.

Which never came.

The two guards were still standing in the guardhouse, slump-shouldered, staring down at their phones. Birds chirped in the trees. Wind rustled leaves.

"We're wasting time," said Jake.

"No," said Kojo. "We're executing our Naranhi Seogi stance. Means we're ready for anything, baby."

"I know what a Naranhi Seogi is," said Jake. "It's also known as a ready stance. And your fists should only be six inches away from your navel, Kojo, not eight."

"Oh. Suddenly you know tae kwon do? Did one of Farooqi's jelly beans come from Korea? Because I thought he lived in New Jersey."

"Sorry. Sometimes my brain goes into TMI overload."

"Tell me about it."

"Let's check out the door."

Jake gestured toward the plain door cut into the front of the colossal building. There was a small, glowing rectangle above its doorknob. "I want to examine that keypad before we go."

"Probably need to punch in some kind of security code," said Kojo as he and Jake crouch-ran to the doorway.

Kojo was correct. The screen was filled with a glowing image:

A red box with a thick black border. A red square without a border. A red circle with a thick black border. A *green* square with the same border as the first red square. A small red square with a black border boxing it in.

There were no instructions.

Just two words etched into the metal plate framing the screen: VIRTUOSO VILLAGE.

"This is it," said Jake. "The home of the Virtuoso quantum computer. I'm guessing it's using its advanced artificial intelligence to operate Tweedle. Lulu is the command and data input portal."

"So everything we're looking for is behind that locked door?" said Kojo.

"Correct."

"So tap in the code, baby. Open it!"

Jake nodded. "I would if I could. But there aren't any instructions. No puzzle. No code to crack." He gestured at the glowing symbols. "I have absolutely no idea what I'm supposed to do."

47

"You have no idea?" said Kojo. "Seriously?"

"Seriously." Jake snapped a photo of the puzzle.

"Oh, I get it. We've gone from TMI to NIAA—no information at all?"

"Yeah."

"You need those new jelly beans."

"Maybe. I also need to—"

Jake was cut off by sharp, metallic growling.

GRRAAAW! GRRAAAW! GRRAAAW!

He and Kojo whirled around.

A trio of clicking, clacking robotic bears with glowing potbellies circled them, their servos whirring.

"Three giant Lulus!" shouted Kojo.

"Only angrier," added Jake.

The six-foot-tall bloated polar bears had the same stylized faces as the smaller virtual assistant versions. But these ginormous, rubbery bears could tilt back their heads and snap open their faces to reveal jagged rows of very sharp, very pointy, very glisteny metal teeth.

"The Lulu in my cabin doesn't have teeth!" said Kojo.

"Mine neither!" said Jake.

They backed up against each other as the three robotic bears tightened their circle.

"Why do I feel like a bowl of porridge right now?" said Kojo.

Suddenly, the three bears' black eye dots glowed green. They became targeting lasers that pinpointed Jake and Kojo where it would really hurt.

Jake chanced a glance over to the guardhouse. The two humans were still staring down at their phones. Apparently, the security cameras and the artificial intelligence controlling Zinkle's security had summoned a more reliable strike force—the three mechanical Lulus.

The bears echoed their synchronized growl.

GRRAAAW! GRRAAAW! GRRAAAW!

Then one bear started talking! It had the same very pleasant, very soothing female voice of the artificially intelligent Lulu in Jake's cabin.

"Please step away from the door. Please step away from the door."

Next came a loud thumping noise.

But not from the bears.

No. A helicopter was landing. Right on the circular patch of asphalt in front of building eleven. Its eggbeater rotor blades were whomping and whirling and whipping up the wind.

The guards in the security shack remained oblivious to the helicopters and the robo-bears. Their eyes were glued to their Tweedle screens. One even looked like he was attempting to do a few dance moves in the cramped hut. (Either that or he just wanted to punch the ceiling.)

The chopper's side door slid open as its skids touched down.

Grace Garcia, her long black hair floating wildly in the rotors' downdraft, braced herself in the doorway.

"Sorry we're a little late," she hollered. "They picked me up at school first. Hurry! Those bears look hungry!"

"They're robots!" shouted Jake. "They don't eat."

"Oh yeah?" shouted Kojo. "They sure look like they want to take a bite out of our butts."

Kojo took off running. Jake was half a step behind him.

The robo-bears?

They lumbered and waddled forward as they snapped their jaws and swallowed a lot of empty air.

Running wasn't exactly the clumsy mechanical beasts' superpower. They didn't even have legs. Just swivel wheels underneath their roly-poly bodies.

As soon as Jake and Kojo leapt in, Grace slid the helicopter door shut with a sideways slam. Jake and Kojo strapped themselves in. Grace redid her seat belt and tapped the back of the pilot's seat.

"Go! Go!"

The chopper lifted off, leaving the robo-bears and the Zinkleplex behind.

For a little while, anyhow.

Jake knew they'd be coming back.

Soon.

But first he needed to test some fresh jelly beans, analyze a few marshmallows, and figure out what was up with that entry-code puzzle for building eleven.

48

Jake's mother's day was almost as busy as her son's.

"Ms. McQuade?" said Arturo, one of the hardest workers on her banquet staff. "Should we put the video screens for Dr. Blackbridge in the usual spots?"

"Yes, please. And make sure there are a few bottles of room-temperature water in the podium. Dr. Blackbridge prefers Fiji Water."

"You got it, Ms. McQuade."

"Thanks, Arturo."

Jake's mother had already consulted with the chef about that evening's four-course dinner. Everything from soup and appetizers to dinner and dessert. Six different kinds of dessert!

Smelling all the delicious aromas wafting around in the Imperial Marquis Hotel's busy kitchen reminded Jake's mother that she hadn't had lunch. Just an energy bar for breakfast.

She was starving.

"Yo, Michelle."

Tony, who, sad to say, was probably the laziest employee on Ms. McQuade's staff, came into the cavernous kitchen carrying a small cellophane-wrapped gift basket.

"Where you want I should put this?" Tony asked.

"What is it?"

Tony shrugged. "Not sure. Looks like a gift basket." He rustled the clear plastic wrap. "Chocolate-covered marshmallows. Like those Easter bunnies, only these don't look like rabbits, just marshmallows."

"Who's it for?"

Tony shrugged again. "Don't know. Courier dropped it off at the loading dock. I was on my break."

Tony took a lot of breaks.

"In fact," he said, "my break isn't over for five more minutes, so . . ."

Ms. McQuade sighed. "I'll take care of it."

"Thanks, Michelle. You're a sweetie."

Tony handed her the gift basket and casually strolled back to the loading dock to loaf.

Jake's mother knew she should have a word with Tony. About his work ethic. And tucking in his shirt. But mostly about not calling your boss "Michelle" or "sweetie."

Unfortunately, all that would have to wait for a less frantic day. There was still too much to do before the reception started at six p.m.

Dr. Sinclair Blackbridge was that night's guest speaker. He was the most eminent futurist in the world. The ballroom would be packed with very important people, dignitaries eager to hear what Dr. Blackbridge thought the "next big thing" might be. The last time he spoke at the hotel, it had been Ingestible Knowledge. Jake's mother had worked that night, too.

To be honest, she thought the idea of getting smart by swallowing some kind of capsules or pills would never happen. But, then again, she wasn't the world's most famous futurist.

Ms. McQuade glanced at the gift card attached to the cellophane wrapping:

ENJOY! THANKS FOR EVERYTHING.
Zane Zinkle

Well, what do you know, she thought. *It's for me!*

Zane Zinkle had sent her a thank-you gift for allowing Jake to attend his Genius Camp. How very thoughtful. And sweet.

Since she'd skipped lunch and probably wouldn't eat dinner, Jake's mother eagerly tore open the pretty cellophane wrapping and quickly devoured one of the chocolate-covered marshmallows. It was delicious. So she ate another one. And then a third.

Buzzing from the chocolate and sugar, she felt ready for anything.

Especially a nap.

Yes, she thought, *a nap would be good.*

She headed for the greenroom. The place where speakers waited before they went into the ballroom to give their talks. There was a couch in the greenroom. And a table where she could eat the rest of the yummy marshmallows.

A full dozen.

When the marshmallows were all gone, she licked every speck of melted chocolate off her fingertips.

And then she stretched out on the couch and started giggling.

Because she was remembering a joke Jake had told her years ago.

Why should you never fart on an elevator?

Because it's just wrong on so many levels.

She closed her eyes. She had time to take a little nap.

She *needed* a little nap.

When she woke up, she thought she might go hang out on the loading dock with Tony.

That'd be fun.

Tony probably knew some pretty funny fart jokes.

49

"**O**h my," said Farooqi. "These marshmallows are bad, my young friends. Very, very bad!"

Jake, Kojo, and Grace had landed at a private airfield in New Jersey, where a waiting limousine had whisked them to Haazim Farooqi's lab. (Jake was so glad the judge gave Grace all that treasure. It made transportation super easy.)

Before even talking about the new batch of jelly beans, Jake wanted Farooqi to test the chocolate-covered treats he'd smuggled out of Genius Camp. Farooqi spent several hours dipping the "suspect material," as he called it, into all sorts of chemicals and studying the bubbles and vapors they emitted.

He sliced off slivers of marshmallow to spin in a microfilter centrifuge. He studied samples on glass slides underneath his electron microscope and with what he called a "spectroscopy whoozeewhatzit."

"At least these marshmallows are kosher and halal, much like my jelly beans," he announced.

"What do you mean?" asked Grace.

"Their creator used fish gelatin, as do I. But that is where any similarity ends." He whipped off his goggles dramatically. "These marshmallows are the bizarro versions of my jelly beans."

"Bizarro?" said Grace.

"From the Bizarro World comic books," said Jake. "On the cube-shaped planet Htrae, everything is the opposite or mirror image of what it would be on Earth."

"Bizarro, the supervillain, had the opposite powers of Superman," added Kojo. "My dad has a mint *Superman* number eighty-eight in his comic book collection. 'Fall of Bizarro!' Even the DC Comics logo is backward on the cover."

"Whoever created these confections," said Farooqi, "set out to do the opposite of what I had hoped to achieve with my jelly beans. If you eat enough of these marshmallows, your intelligence will undoubtedly be impaired."

"Permanently?" asked Grace.

Farooqi could only shrug. "Unfortunately, my analysis cannot answer that question."

"How about you, Jake?" said Grace. "Can you answer it?"

"No. I wish I could. But I can't."

"Don't worry," said Kojo. "You will soon enough. You just need a jelly bean boost, baby!"

"Ah, yes," said Farooqi. He pulled open a filing cabinet drawer and proudly presented a hinged-top jar filled with brightly colored jelly beans.

"Whoa," said Kojo. "That's a whole lot of Ingestible Knowledge."

"Eight ounces," said Farooqi. "One half pound of pure IK deliciousness."

"Is that how much you ate the first time?" wondered Grace.

"Maybe," said Jake, sort of embarrassed. "I remember I was extremely hungry."

"There are eight different colors, eight different flavors," said Farooqi. "Eight different formulations."

"Do you know which ones do what?" asked Kojo.

"No. Not really. But eat eight, one of each color, and you're pretty much covered in all major fields of study. Eat them all, the entire jar of jelly beans? Well, then you become Jake McQuade. The smartest kid in the universe."

"And if *I* eat some of these on top of the ones I already ate?" asked Jake.

"We can assume," said Farooqi, "that, just like squaring or cubing a number, your mental powers will expand exponentially."

Farooqi brought the jar over to a worktable and unclasped the lid.

"This is everything I have made thus far," he said. "They are yours, Subject One. Use them wisely."

"Did you remember to write down the formula this time?"

"Yes," said Farooqi. "Most of it. I think. I know I had a pen and a pad of paper. I had completed a doodle of a donkey sporting a mustache. . . ."

Jake smiled and shook his head. "I'll try the licorice." He plucked out a black bean.

"That's one small bean for two fingers," said Farooqi, "one giant leap for bean-kind!"

Everybody else arched their eyebrows and gave him a puzzled look.

"Sorry. Sometimes I get a little carried away."

"You want us to give you another drumroll?" asked Kojo.

"No thank you. Not necessary."

Jake moved the jelly bean to his mouth.

"One minute," said Farooqi. "I might want to post this on my podcast at beans4brains.net, if I ever do a podcast." He whipped out a small recorder and started dictating into it. "Three-thirty-three post meridiem time in the Eastern time zone of the United States of America, located in the Northern Hemisphere of the planet currently known as Earth. Subject One is about to ingest the black IK capsule, which should increase his mental capacity for . . ."

He riffled through a small spiral notebook.

"Uh . . . miscellaneous and obscure knowledge about, uh, stuff. Very good for party games, trivia, and visual puzzles. I think. Maybe."

In other words, Farooqi had no idea what this particular jelly bean might do.

Jake closed his eyes and tossed the jelly bean into his mouth.

50

The licorice jelly bean was crunchy on the outside, squishy on the inside.

It didn't taste too bad, either. Not all the way to a Jelly Belly, but very edible.

Wait a second.

All of a sudden, Jake knew that Goelitz, the maker of Jelly Belly candies, was named after Gustav Goelitz, a German immigrant who settled in Illinois in 1866 and popularized a form of "mallow melt" he called "chicken feed" but soon became known as "candy corn," the classic Halloween treat.

"Eureka!" Jake shouted. "I think it worked. I know some junk I didn't know before. For instance, there is a Tabasco-flavored Jelly Belly."

Kojo blew air out of the side of his mouth. "*Pfft*. I could've told you that."

Mr. Farooqi clapped his hands together. Tears welled up in his eyes.

"It worked?" he asked, his voice quivering. "I mean . . ." He tried to act confident and made a triumphant gesture. "It worked! Huzzah!"

"You're even smarter?" Grace asked Jake. "Are you sure?"

"Yeah. I think so."

Jake fumbled for his phone and checked the photo he'd taken of that security pad screen.

Jake smiled.

"Oh yeah," he said. "The bean is definitely working. I'm pretty sure I now know how to get into building eleven!"

51

Jake, Kojo, and Grace piled back into the waiting limousine.

"Waiting time costs extra, am I right?" said Kojo.

"Yes," said Grace. "But it doesn't matter."

Kojo shot her a wink. "Spoken like the richest kid in the world."

"Let's just go."

"As you wish, Miss Garcia," said the chauffeur.

The car pulled out of the New Jersey college campus's parking lot.

A muffled *DINKLE-DINK, DINKLE-DINK* alert sounded inside a zippered pocket on Grace's backpack.

"What was that?" asked Jake.

"Uncle Charley's zPhone. I had to take it away from him. He was Tweedling twenty-four-seven."

"Did you delete the app?"

"Of course," said Grace, fishing out the device. She tapped the screen and the zPhone woke up.

Grace gasped.

"What?" said Kojo. "What are you gasping about?"

Grace showed her friends the zPhone's home screen.

"That was a push alert. Tweedle is gone. But there are two new apps that I did not download. Flimflam and Hoodwink."

"Oh, nice icon for Hoodwink, there," said Kojo. "A winking Robin Hood emoji . . ."

"Don't open those, Grace," Jake warned. "Tweedle probably knows when it's been deleted and spawns two similar, maybe even stronger apps to replace itself."

"And if we delete these two," said Grace, "that'll probably spread to four evil apps."

"All those Tweedle apps you deleted at school . . ."

Grace nodded. "They've just morphed into two new mind-warping apps. Forget the helicopter, we need to stay in town. Go to school tomorrow. Try to confiscate everybody's zPhones."

Jake shook his head. "No. Nobody would willingly part with their devices. Especially if Tweedle, Hoodwink, and Flimflam have been brainwashing them for days. We need to nip this thing in the bud. We need to get inside building eleven and, somehow, disable the Virtuoso computer. It's how Zinkle runs all this."

"You know how to crack the code on the security pad?" said Kojo. "Because back at Farooqi's, you said you did. But when we were right outside building eleven, you said you didn't."

"The new black bean helped clarify things," said Jake. "I'm pretty sure it's an 'odd one out' quiz. They're pretty standard on IQ tests. For instance, which one doesn't belong: tree, mouse, paper, man?"

"I'm going to say paper," said Kojo. "It's the only non-living thing."

"Correct! Here's another: a triangle, a square, the letter 'E,' and the letter 'M.'"

Kojo rubbed his face with his hand to think.

"The triangle," said Grace. "It's the odd one out because it only has three line segments. The square, the 'E,' and the 'M' all have four."

"You are also correct," said Jake.

"But that thing on the screen wasn't as easy," said Kojo.

"I didn't think mine was so easy," said Grace. "Sure, yours was. . . ."

Jake lit up his phone to take another look at the picture he'd snapped of the security panel puzzle:

While he was trying to find the "odd one out," the phone started braying its most annoying ringtone: *"I've*

got a friend, my friend's calling me," sang an obnoxiously nasal voice, *"yeah-uh, yeah-uh, you haven't got one, no-wee, no-wee . . ."*

It was his custom alert for his little sister, Emma (who sometimes could be super annoying).

"Emma?" Jake said. "We're kind of busy and . . ."

Jake froze. He didn't say a word. He just listened in what looked like shock.

"What's wrong?" asked Grace.

52

Jake didn't answer Grace right away.

"Yo?" said Kojo. "Earth to Jake. You're scarin' us."

Finally, Jake spoke.

"Don't worry, Emma," he said into his phone. "We're on our way. Keep telling Mom fart jokes. There's a whole book of them in my bedroom. On the bottom shelf of my bookcase. Hang tight, Emma. We'll be there as quickly as we can."

"What's up?" said Kojo when Jake ended the call.

"My mom. They sent her home from work early because she ate some of Zinkle's marshmallows and started telling everybody, including her boss, fart jokes."

"For real?" asked Grace.

"She was in the background while I was talking to Emma," said Jake. "She kept yelling for me to bring her 'more of those yummy chocolate marshmallows' Mr.

Zinkle sent her at work. Emma says Mom's acting worse than I used to. She's already sprayed a whole can of Cheez Whiz straight into her mouth. She used a couch cushion for a napkin. Emma's afraid to let her go into the bathroom. Who knows what she might use for toilet paper?"

Grace powered down the divider window separating the back of the limo from the front.

"Driver? Change of plans."

She gave the chauffeur the address for Jake's apartment.

"And hurry!"

Making sure Jake's mother was okay?

It took priority over everything else.

The limousine exited the New Jersey Turnpike and headed into the city. The helicopter would wait overnight at the private airfield.

But the drone that had been tracking Jake, Kojo, and Grace ever since they'd left the Zinkleplex?

It didn't follow them.

It kept transmitting the coordinates of Haazim Farooqi's laboratory to Lulu and the Virtuoso quantum computer humming away inside building eleven.

53

"You know how the ocean says hello?" Jake's mother asked him with a goofy grin on her face.

"Yes, Mom," said Jake. "It waves."

Jake, Grace, and Kojo had been at Jake's apartment for several hours. The way Jake's mother was acting reminded him of what had happened to Christina up at Genius Camp.

"Hey, Jake?"

"Yeah, Mom?"

"Why do birds fly south in the winter?"

"Because it's easier than walking."

His mother gave Jake a pouting, party-pooper look. "You knew that one, too? Okay. Why did Jake's mother stop telling fart jokes?"

"Because everybody told her they stink."

"You're no fun," said his mother. "You're too smart. You know the answers to everything."

Except, Jake thought, what the antidote might be to Zane Zinkle's brain-draining chocolate-covered marshmallows. The things were like squishy zombies. They wanted your braaaains. He'd been racking his own brain, trying to come up with a solution. So far, he had nothing. What good was being the smartest kid in the universe if he couldn't even help his own mother?

"Come on, Ms. McQ," said Kojo. "It's nearly three a.m. Let's go into the living room and watch a little TV. There are all sorts of boring infomercials on at this hour. Maybe we can find one to put you to sleep."

"Okay, Kojo," slurred Jake's mother, sounding like her marshmallow buzz was finally wearing off. She was staring down at her slippers. "Can you remind me: Which one is my left foot and which one is my right?"

"Doesn't really matter right now, Ms. McQ. Just shuffle them forward, one at a time, till we reach the couch. There you go. Nice and easy . . ."

Kojo helped Jake's mother into the living room.

"Emma?" said Jake. "You should go to bed. We've got this."

"It's so scary," said Emma, sniffling a little. She was all cried out. "Mom's so different. She reminds me of you, Jake."

Jake cracked a smile. "Thanks, sis," he said softly.

"Not now. But, you know. Before you had your brain spurt or whatever."

"You're right. Now go to bed. Grace, Kojo, and I will keep an eye on Mom."

"Okay. I'll try. And, Jake?"

"Yeah?"

"Thanks again."

Exhausted, Emma slouched off to her bedroom.

Grace and Kojo had already called their parents, let them know that they "had another situation" to deal with. Ever since Grace, Kojo, and Jake had outwitted the bad guys and found the treasure buried underneath their middle school, their families all believed and trusted them when they said they had to deal with something super serious.

Grace and Jake headed into the kitchen and sat down at the table.

"You can take Mom's room," said Jake. "Kojo can have mine. I'll roll out my sleeping bag in the living room, keep an eye on Mom."

"And then what? What do we do when we wake up— if we can even fall asleep?"

Jake rubbed both of his temples. "I'm not sure."

54

Neither Jake nor Grace were ready for bed.

So they had a snack. Cookies and milk for Jake. Ice cream for Grace.

"So, what's Zinkle doing at school?" Grace wondered. "Why'd he adopt Riverview?"

"I'm not sure," said Jake. "Maybe we're some kind of test market. If his apps can make all the students and teachers do and buy all sorts of weird and useless stuff . . ."

Grace picked up on Jake's chain of thought. "Then Zinkle Inc. and its artificially intelligent, constantly changing, app-delivered, brainwashing algorithms can sell anything to anybody anywhere."

"It'd be every advertiser's dream come true," said Jake.

"We should all buy stock in snap bracelets," Grace said sarcastically.

Jake laughed. Just a little. "Our best bet for saving the school and preventing Zinkle from taking this thing global—maybe our only hope—is to disable the servers. To bring down Virtuoso. We need to pull the plug on Zinkle's hyperprocessing quantum computer."

"And how exactly do we do that?"

"I'm not sure. But it starts with sneaking into building eleven. That's Virtuoso's home."

"I'll call the chopper people. Reserve a ride for first thing tomorrow." She stretched into a yawn. Jake thought it was a very attractive yawn.

Not that he'd ever tell Grace that.

Grace stood up from the table. "Tomorrow's going to be a busy day. We have to help your mother, help Riverview, and, oh yeah, save the world. So right now we both need to get some rest."

"Yeah," said Jake, even though there was a whole bunch of other stuff he wished he could say to Grace. Witty stuff. Suave stuff.

But he had nothing.

Suddenly, his phone started playing the *dee-doo-dee-doo* theme song from *The Twilight Zone*.

Farooqi's ringtone.

"Huh," said Jake. "He's up late."

He tapped the answer icon.

"This is Subject One. What's up, Mr. Farooqi?"

"This is not Mr. Farooqi," said a very creepy but familiar voice. "This is your school's generous sponsor

218

and the gracious host of the Genius Camp where you and your chum Keanu are supposed to be in attendance right now!"

Jake covered the phone. "It's Zinkle."

"What's he doing calling from Mr. Farooqi's phone?" whispered Grace.

Suddenly Jake freaked. If Zinkle had Mr. Farooqi's phone, Mr. Farooqi was probably in trouble.

Kojo strolled into the kitchen. "Your mom's asleep. The pillow guy does it every time, especially when he starts describing the foam and—"

Kojo saw the terrified look on his friend's face.

"What'd I miss?"

Jake put a finger to his lips and went back to the phone call.

"Mr. Zinkle? Why are you calling me on Haazim Farooqi's phone?"

"Because, Jake, your mad-scientist friend is currently my guest. Of course, I didn't give him one of the posh, high-tech, cutting-edge cabins that I gave to you and your friend Kevin. But Mr. Farooqi is here. With me. In my office. Would you like to speak with him?"

"Yes. Please."

"Just a moment."

Jake heard a rustle as Zinkle handed off the phone.

"Greetings, Subject One."

It was Farooqi.

"Sorry to be calling at such a late hour. . . ."

"Are you okay, Mr. Farooqi?"

"Oh yes. So far. But, well, it seems I have been abducted. Perhaps kidnapped."

Jake could hear Farooqi placing his hand over the phone.

"Have I been abducted or kidnapped, Mr. Zinkle?"

There was a second of silence.

"Okay," said Farooqi. "Mr. Zinkle is nodding his head. I was correct. I am an abductee. Also, my lab has once again been destroyed. My notebooks and files and, well, everything. It's all gone. Even my donkey doodles. Mr. Zinkle has some very thorough, very efficient minions."

Jake heard the phone being ripped out of Farooqi's hands.

"You cheated, Jake McQuade!" seethed Zinkle. "I know how you became the smartest kid in the universe. You and Mr. Haazim Farooqi cheated! You two stole what was rightfully mine!"

Jake took a deep breath.

"What do you want, Mr. Zinkle?"

"Are you really that ignorant?" Zinkle said with a chuckle. "Fine. Let me paint you a picture, Jake. I want to cheat like you did. I want the jelly beans. I want them all. And don't you dare tell your friends at the FBI about any of this. If you do, I'll know. And Mr. Farooqi here? Why, he will simply disappear."

"I won't call the FBI," said Jake. "I promise."

"First thing in the morning, bring me the jar Mr. Farooqi gave you and I will let him go. I will also, once again, be much smarter than you! I'll even be smarter than me! In fact, I will be smarter than any human being who has ever walked the face of this planet!"

55

Jake's mother was zonked out, snoring on the couch.

Jake was a little jealous. No way would he be sleeping that soundly tonight (if he slept at all).

He'd slipped inside his sleeping bag, fully clothed. He didn't even take off his socks or sneakers. It was four a.m. He drifted off. For twenty-nine minutes.

At four-thirty, he was staring up at the living room ceiling again, thinking. He'd done a lot of that, of course, ever since he ate that first jar of IK jelly beans in the greenroom of the Imperial Marquis Hotel on that fateful night.

Jake wasn't having any deep, brilliant, or even halfway interesting thoughts. All he could think about was what he had done.

To his mother.

His friends at school.

Haazim Farooqi. Poor guy. He'd not only lost his life's

work but now his life was in serious jeopardy. Zane Zinkle had revealed himself to be a dangerous, maybe even psychotic player. Mr. Farooqi could get hurt. Or worse.

And what about Abia Sulayman? She'd been so smart. She'd played Lemoncello games at the highest level. Now? She didn't seem to care about anything, except maybe winning a burping contest.

Dawn Yang, Poindexter Perkins, Mackenzie Meekleman, they'd all eaten the chocolate marshmallows and suffered the consequences. Zinkle did something to the Genius Camp counselors, Todd and Christina, too.

This was worse than losing his own brainy superpowers.

What was it Grace had said? *We are given our talents to help others. Not ourselves.*

Turns out, Jake was given his talents to hurt others.

Four-fifty.

Jake dozed for another twenty minutes.

Five-ten.

He stared at the clock. Watched its digits flip to eleven . . . twelve . . .

He needed sleep. He'd be going up against Zane Zinkle first thing in the morning. Jake would need to fortify his brain for the coming conflict. He'd gobble down the new jelly beans. The whole jar.

But he couldn't do that. Zinkle wanted the jelly beans. He needed them to free Farooqi. So maybe he'd only eat a few . . .

Jake decided to count jelly beans instead of sheep.

Eight colors. Eight flavors.

How many sets of eight were in the jar?

Jake tried to reconstruct the jar in his head. Eight. Sixteen. Twenty-four. Thirty-two. Forty . . .

Wait a second.

There are eight different colors, eight different flavors, Farooqi had said. *Eight different formulations. Eat eight, one of each color, and you're pretty much covered in all major fields of study.*

Jake smiled and took one last glance at the clock.

He'd sleep till six. Maybe six-thirty.

And then he'd wake up and make his mother breakfast.

Because, suddenly, he knew exactly how to use his talents to help others. All the victims of Zinkle's brain-draining.

If it worked.

First thing in the morning, his mother would become Subject One in a new field test.

Because Jake was going to feed her eight delicious jelly beans for breakfast.

One of each color and flavor.

56

"Um, Jake?" said Emma. "Why are you serving Mom jelly beans for breakfast?"

"That's okay, honey," said their mother. "I like candy. Especially for breakfast. Hey, Jake—do you know what kind of bear has no teeth?"

"A gummy bear, Mom."

"That's right!" his mother said with a laugh and a knee slap. "That's hysterical! Woo. Woo. A gummy bear!" She laughed so hard, she had tears in her eyes. She wiped them dry with a paper napkin that she also used to blow her nose. "Hey, Jakey-Wakey, how about instead of jelly beans, I have some more of those marshmallows that Mr. Zinkle sent to the hotel? He's such a nice man. . . ."

"Nah, Ms. McQ," said Kojo. "The jelly beans are better for breakfast. Some of them are even fruit flavored."

"That orange one?" said Grace. "It's just like chewing orange juice."

Emma rolled her eyes. She had no idea why her big brother and his supersmart friends were acting like such idiots. Jake, of course, had filled Grace and Kojo in on the hypothesis for his experiment. He'd also chewed through seven more jelly beans himself—every color in the jar except black, because he'd already ingested that one.

With sixteen beans missing, the jar still looked full. There'd be enough for Zinkle when they delivered his ransom demand. Enough to free Mr. Farooqi.

"Mmm. That one tasted like a pineapple," said Jake's mom, chewing her second jelly bean. "Which is what you get when you cross a computer with a Christmas tree."

"Heh-heh-heh," Kojo fake-laughed. "Good one, Ms. McQ. Good one."

"Have another jelly bean, Mom," coached Jake.

"Are you kids sure this is what I should be eating for breakfast?"

"Oh yeah," said Kojo. "It's National Jelly Bean Awareness Day. Somewhere."

Jake's mom, who did have a sweet tooth, popped the rest of the jelly beans into her mouth.

"Delicious," she said. "But, guys? There is no such thing as National Jelly Bean Awareness Day. And so much sugar for breakfast is never a good idea. You'll just crash in a couple hours. That's why I always try to serve oatmeal or eggs, if there's time."

Jake, Grace, and Kojo smiled at each other.

"Um, what are you guys smiling about?" asked Jake's mother.

"Nothing," said Jake. "It's just great to have you back. I mean to be back. From camp. But now, uh, we have to go back. *To* camp. Grace is coming with us."

"Hey, Mom," said Emma, "why did you stop telling fart jokes?"

"Excuse me?"

"You stopped telling them because they stink!"

Jake's mother glared at Emma.

"Are you done, young lady?"

"Yes, Mom."

"Good. Because this is not the time or place for that kind of crude humor."

"You're right!" said Emma. Then she sprang up out of her chair and gave her mother a great big hug. She squeezed so tight, it looked like she might never let go.

"Well, we gotta run," said Jake. "Camp calls."

"This Genius Camp is the strangest sleepover camp I've ever heard of," said his mother after giving Emma a kiss on her forehead. "You don't really sleep over very much, do you?"

"Because we wanted to have breakfast with you!" said Kojo.

"See you later, Ms. McQuade," said Grace. "Oh, you might want to check in with work before you go. See if anybody, you know, is talking about anything."

That earned Grace a very confused look.

"Don't worry, Mom," said Emma. "Arturo covered your butt."

"What? Why did my butt need covering? Emma?"

"Later, guys," said Jake.

He had enough to worry about. Emma could be in charge of explaining to their mom what happened yesterday at the Imperial Marquis Hotel when she told her boss a string of fart jokes and was asked to go home early.

57

Grace summoned another chauffeur.

"You need a more permanent driver," said Kojo. "Somebody named Jeeves or Chauncy."

"This is only temporary," explained Grace. "Until we rescue Mr. Farooqi and disable the evil app monster."

"It's not a monster," said Jake. "It's just an evilly programmed computer."

The three friends climbed into the back of the stretch limousine.

"Nice," said Kojo, admiring the posh interior.

Grace gave the driver the address for Zinkle's World Headquarters. He said, "Yes, ma'am," and rolled up the privacy window.

The limo started its cruise north.

"What about the driver?" Jake whispered. "Bringing an adult into this might spook Zinkle. He could overreact and 'disappear' Mr. Farooqi."

"He'll wait at the gate," Grace whispered back.

"You're gonna rack up even more waiting time?" said Kojo.

"I guess," said Grace.

"And you know they charge for waiting time?"

"So you keep reminding me."

Kojo held up both hands and shrugged. "Just saying. You're gonna lose that 'richest kid in the world' hashtag big-time."

"We both might lose our titles if Zinkle gets his hands on these," said Jake, stuffing the lidded jar of jelly beans down into his backpack.

"Nah," said Kojo. "He can't be the smartest kid in the universe. He's over eighteen. There's rules about these things."

"We should call Uncle Charley," said Grace. "See how things are going at school."

"Good idea," said Jake. "Hopefully everybody's not so far gone that nothing we do will help them."

"Wait a second," said Kojo. "We're not just going back to Genius Camp to rescue Mr. Farooqi?"

"That's our primary objective," said Jake. "But once we have him, I say we still go pay a little visit to building eleven."

"You're playing that three-dimensional chess in your head again, aren't you?"

Jake couldn't help but grin. "Maybe. Call your uncle Charley, Grace. Let's hope we're not too late to turn things around at Riverview."

"Put him on speaker," urged Kojo.

Grace nodded and placed the call.

"Hello?" came the anxious answer.

"Uncle Charley? It's Grace. I'm with Kojo and Jake."

"How's it going, Coach Lyons?" asked Kojo.

"Things are bad," said Mr. Lyons. "Thank goodness you confiscated my phone, Grace. Everyone else's zPhones have become infected with new apps. Hoodwink. Flim-flam. Dupe."

"Dupe?" said Grace. "That one's new."

"Apparently it sets fashion trends. Everybody, except me, is wearing plaid on plaid. Plaid shirts and plaid pants. Plaid blouses with plaid skirts and plaid knee-high socks."

"Hang in there, Uncle Charley," said Grace. "With any luck, all of this will be over by the end of the day."

"I sure hope so. My eyes hurt."

Grace nodded. "Too much plaid will do that to you."

She said goodbye and ended the call.

Kojo turned to Jake. "And you said this thing isn't a monster. Plaid on plaid? That's just wrong, man."

"Virtuoso is testing the outer limits of its influencer power," said Jake. "Seeing if it can generate a full-on fashion fad. Like those goofy sneakers everybody was wearing last year."

Kojo casually tucked his feet under the bench seat so no one could see his shoes. Grace did, too.

"Grace?" said Jake. "We need to make one more stop."

"Where?"

"A supermarket. Any place they sell jelly beans and decorative glass jars."

58

When the limo arrived at the Zinkle headquarters, there were no guards in the gatehouse.

But the entrance bridge over the moat was blocked by a barricade. Thick steel bars poked up through the arched concrete roadway at its midpoint.

Grace tapped the privacy window. The driver rolled it down.

"Please wait here," she told him.

"We charge for that."

"We know!" said Jake and Grace. (Kojo had an *I told you so* look on his face.)

Jake, Grace, and Kojo piled out of the limo and made their way up the wide driveway toward the colossal glass headquarters building looming on the horizon.

Jake was carrying the new jar of jelly beans he'd put together in the parking lot of a ShopRite supermarket.

Hopefully, he wouldn't have to give up Mr. Farooqi's actual jar of IK capsules. If this worked, all Zane Zinkle would be gobbling down would be one pound of assorted-flavor Jelly Bellys.

"Weird," said Grace as they strolled past the empty guardhouse.

"It'll probably get weirder," said Kojo. "Things up here usually do."

"But where did the guards go?"

"If I had to guess," said Jake, "Zinkle has switched to some sort of fully automated security system. No humans. Just machines. Machines are easier to control and manipulate than people."

"Unless you feed those people chocolate-covered marshmallows," said Kojo.

Jake nodded. Zane Zinkle had manipulated the other genius campers into lumpy shadows of their formerly brilliant selves. He'd wanted to do the same to Jake and Kojo. It was only Jake's not-so-fond memory of those Easter basket Peeps that had saved them.

When the three friends reached the center of the bridge, the whole glass building—still one hundred feet in front of them—started to glow. The windows were illuminated by a slowly shifting rainbow of colors. The saucer dome up top went milky white with projections of a trapezoidal black nose and two black dots for eyes.

"Check it out," said Kojo. "Zinkle's turned his

whole headquarters building into a giant four-story-tall Lulu!"

"What's a Lulu?" asked Grace.

"Kind of like a polar bear–shaped Alexa," explained Jake.

"Only sometimes," said Kojo, "especially right outside building eleven, Lulu has razor-sharp teeth."

"Riiight," said Grace, remembering seeing the three roly-poly bears that chased Kojo and Jake onto her helicopter.

"I think Lulu is also Mr. Zinkle's access portal to the Virtuoso quantum computer," said Jake. "He has one sitting on his office desk."

They reached the steel bars in the middle of the bridge.

"Welcome back to the Zinkleplex," boomed Lulu's calm voice.

"Whoa," said Kojo. "The whole building is talking. This is, like, the world's biggest doorbell camera."

"I see you have brought the IK capsules and your friends," Lulu continued. "Kojo Shelton and Grace Garcia."

"How'd you know my name?" demanded Grace.

"Simple data mining," said Lulu. "I believe you gave Zinkle Incorporated full access to all your personal information during your most recent zPhone software update."

"I just clicked the box at the end of a mile-long scroll of tiny words nobody ever reads."

"And that's all we needed. How are those blue jeans you bought on Tuesday working out for you?"

"Ignore Lulu," said Jake. He held up the jar with the ordinary jelly beans. "I brought Mr. Zinkle what he wants. Where's Mr. Farooqi?"

"With Mr. Zinkle," Lulu calmly replied.

"So, can you, you know, lower these bars? We need to exchange this jar for Haazim Farooqi."

"Would you like to play a game?" asked the building.

"Um, excuse me?"

"Would you like to play a game?"

"Sure," said Jake. "As soon as Mr. Farooqi is free and we're all done with the ransom and junk."

"Would you like to play a game?"

"Right now?"

"Yes. If you win, Jake McQuade, I will lower the steel bars as you recently requested. You can then proceed to the next level."

Jake looked to his two friends.

"I told you this would get weirder," Kojo told Grace out of the corner of his mouth.

"Go for it, Jake," said Grace. "You've outplayed Virtuoso before."

It was true. Jake had defeated the quantum computer's artificial intelligence during the Zinkle Extreme Masters Tournament at his mother's hotel.

He might be able to do it again.

After all, he'd gobbled down a whole booster set of eight jelly beans.

"And what do *you* get if I lose?" Jake shouted up at the glowing building.

"Nothing from you, Jake McQuade," Lulu replied pleasantly. "Just total control and continued domination of all your friends back at Riverview Middle School and, eventually, the world."

59

Kojo used his hand to shield his voice from Lulu's listening devices.

"It's okay. You'll win. Probably."

"But," whispered Grace, "if you lose, we definitely need to race back to school and snag everybody's zPhones, whether they like it or not."

Suddenly, behind Jake and his friends, another series of sharp steel bars rose out of the bridge's concrete pavement—maybe ten feet away from the guardhouse.

"Okay," said Kojo, "so much for racing back to school. We're trapped."

"If you don't lower at least one set of these bars," demanded Grace, "I will instruct my driver to call the police."

"I'm afraid he is no longer your driver, Miss Garcia," said Lulu smoothly.

Jake heard a car engine start up and the limo pull away.

"It seems," said Lulu, "that the limousine company just sent your driver a text commanding him to return to base. Apparently, your credit card has been rejected."

"You did that!" shouted Kojo, pointing an accusing finger at the glimmering glass box.

"Brilliant deduction, Mr. Shelton. Perhaps your dreams will come true and you will be a detective mastermind when you grow up."

"Don't try to butter me up, Lulu," snapped Kojo. "Let's play whatever game you've got up your sleeve, or your elevator shaft, seeing how, all of a sudden, you're a whole building instead of a roly-poly rubber bear."

"Are you ready to proceed, Jake McQuade?"

Jake nodded.

"Let the games begin," added Grace. She sounded like she was still mad about Lulu tapping into her personal data, canceling her credit card, and sending away her driver.

"Very well," Lulu purred smugly.

There was some tinkling chime music, and several windows on the four-story-tall headquarters building lit up to create a square box broken into a four-by-four grid. There were two smaller squares over the grid's vertical center line: one where it intersected with the first horizontal line down from the top, another where it intersected with the third horizontal line down.

"How many squares do you see, Jake?" asked Lulu. "You have sixty seconds to answer correctly."

"Oh, man," moaned Kojo. "It looks like a chunky basketball court."

"I think I saw this puzzle on the internet," said Grace. "I couldn't solve it then, either."

"Okay, Jake," said Kojo, launching into the kind of pep talk Coach Lyons usually gave them on the basketball sidelines. "Let's show Lulu we came to play. You're never a loser until you quit trying. You miss all the shots you don't take. Uh, tuck in your jersey. . . ."

Jake didn't say anything. He was too busy. Focusing. Doing the math.

"You have thirty seconds remaining," announced

Lulu. "And kindly remember that I am looking for the total number of squares, not rectangles, even though a square, by definition is also a rectangle and—"

"Yo!" Kojo shouted up at the glass building. "My man's thinking. He does that better when nobody's talking trash in his face."

"I'm sorry if you think—"

"The correct answer is forty squares," Jake declared. "I count eight tiny squares, eighteen single squares, nine two-by-two squares, four three-by-three squares, and, of course, one big four-by-four square."

All was quiet.

Until the bars blocking the way forward receded into the bridge. Then there were a lot of grating steel-screeching-on-concrete noises.

"Kindly proceed to your next challenge," said Lulu.

"Oh yeah," Kojo said to Jake. "Lulu really wants to play games with you, bro. Probably because you beat her in that tournament."

Jake realized Kojo might be right. Had the Virtuoso computer's artificial intelligence machine taught itself to seek revenge? Was it craving payback?

"The degree of difficulty of these games is going to increase," Jake told his friends. "Right now, Zane Zinkle is commanding Lulu to analyze my thought processes. To evaluate my tactics. They're sifting and sorting through everything they know about me. They'll use machine learning to design a game I can't win."

"Why?" wondered Grace. "If all Zinkle wants are Mr. Farooqi's jelly beans, why doesn't he just come out and take them? Why make this such a production?"

"I don't know," said Jake.

"I hate when the smartest kid in the universe says that," muttered Kojo.

"But," said Jake, "I do know we're going to need more help."

"Like who?" asked Grace.

"A champion gamer. Someone who's competed at the highest levels under incredible pressure and emerged victorious. We need Abia Sulayman."

60

Jake, Grace, and Kojo raced to the far end of the bridge, where a four-seater golf cart was very conveniently waiting.

"Anybody think this is a coincidence?" said Grace.

"Nope," said Kojo. "I think it's another part of a diabolically clever plan. Plus have you guys noticed? No one else is here. The campus is deserted. The office building looks empty."

"Mr. Zinkle must've given everybody the day off," said Jake.

"Yeah," said Kojo. "It's a holiday. National Kidnap a Neuroscientist Day. Come on. I'll drive. I know the way back to camp."

The three friends hopped into the canopied golf cart. There was a six-inch-tall soft rubber Lulu mounted on the dashboard. Kojo cranked the key in the ignition switch. Nothing happened. He tapped the go pedal. Still nothing.

Except the Lulu started glowing yellow.

"Hello again," said the friendly voice. "To utilize this playing piece, simply answer this question: What are three different whole numbers whose sum and product are equal?"

"Easy," said Grace.

"Um, shouldn't we let the smartest kid in the universe field all the math questions?" said Kojo.

"Not if Grace knows the answer," said Jake. "Hey, both she and you were smart way before my brain woke up."

"It's just so easy," said Grace. "The answer is one, two, and three. One plus two plus three equals six. One times two times three also equals six."

The golf cart lurched forward with a jolt.

"Guess I shouldn't rest my foot on the go pedal," said Kojo, quickly regaining control of the electric vehicle.

"Lulu?" said Jake.

"I'm listening."

"Why'd you call this cart a 'playing piece'?"

"I enjoy games. Don't you?"

"Oh yeah," said Kojo. He grabbed hold of the squishy dashboard Lulu and yanked it up off its suction cups. "One of my favorites is baseball."

He heaved the device as far as he could. It hit the lawn and bounced its way down into the moat.

"I was getting a little tired of her soothing voice," said Kojo. "It's irritating."

"Good arm," said Grace.

"Thanks."

"She'll be back," said Jake. "Those things are every-where up here. But it's probably best that she and Zinkle don't know that we're adding Abia to our team."

"Will Abia be any help?" asked Grace. "You said she ate a ton of those marshmallows."

Jake pulled the jar of Farooqi's jelly beans out of his backpack and gave it a rattle. "Good thing we brought the antidote. Eight of these, hopefully, will bring her back—just like they did with Mom."

Then Jake remembered that there were security cameras all over the Zinkleplex. Especially in the areas designated for Genius Camp activities. He didn't want Zinkle seeing him giving away some of Farooqi's jelly beans. After all, that was their deal. All the jelly beans for Farooqi's freedom. (And, hopefully, it would be all the *fake* IK capsules—the jar of Jelly Bellys.)

"Kojo?" said Jake.

"Yeah?"

"We're gonna need your baseball arm again."

"I play softball," said Grace.

"I didn't know that."

"Guess there's a lot you don't know about me, Jake McQuade."

Jake's ears were suddenly a lot warmer. And it wasn't because of the sun.

"I play center field," said Grace. "I have a wicked throw to the plate."

"That's, um, good to know," said Jake, trying to stop his voice from cracking. "The two of you will be in charge of blinding the security cameras."

"What?" said Kojo. "You want us to chuck rocks at them? Shatter their lenses?"

"No. Marshmallows. Half of their volume is filled with air bubbles created by whipping gelatin into a hot, sugary syrup. When the liquid cools, marshmallows become spongy because of all those bubbles. Hotter temperatures will make the air trapped inside expand and the marshmallows become extremely sticky and gooey."

"The goo will stick to the lenses!" said Grace. "Obstruct their view."

"Exactly. I think it will prove more reliable than rock flinging."

"Totally," said Grace.

The cart cruised through a patch of forest and into the campgrounds. No one was in the dining hall or the picnic pavilion. Finally, Kojo eased the vehicle to a stop near the campfire circle.

Jake made his way over to the big bowl of plastic-wrapped blobs and stuffed as many as he could into his pockets. He hurried back to the golf cart.

"Gimme some of those," said Kojo.

Jake did. Kojo stood up and crammed the marshmallows into the back pockets of his pants. Then he sat back down.

"Doing a little rapid-action thermal transfer," he said.

"Give me some, too," said Grace, standing up and taking two handfuls of marshmallows from Jake. She jammed them into the back pockets of her jeans and sat down. "Oooh. Now, that's what I call a cushioned seat."

"They should be nice and soft by the time we reach the cabins," said Jake.

"Let's roll," said Kojo, tapping the go pedal again. "We need to pick up Abia. And I charge for waiting time, too!"

61

Kojo parked the cart in front of the high-tech cabins.

It was about eleven o'clock in the morning, but no one was out and about. The only sounds were birds chirping.

And snoring.

"Guess that's why they call it sleepaway camp," cracked Grace. "All the campers are still sleeping away the day."

"You guys take out those cameras," said Jake, pointing to two smoky-gray orbs on poles. "I'll go wake up Abia and, hopefully, her brain."

Kojo and Grace chucked their seat-warmed, mushy marshmallows up at the cameras. They were both excellent shots. Their squishy projectiles splatted against the plastic domes, which, because they were tinted dark, had already been warmed by the morning sun. Goop slimed down and blocked Zinkle's view.

Jake bounded up the steps to Abia's cabin and rapped gently on the door.

"Abia? Are you up? It's me. Jake McQuade."

A sleepy-eyed Abia shuffled to the cabin door.

"Why are you knocking at my door so early?" she asked with a yawn.

"I've got something even better than those marshmallows you like so much!" said Jake before Abia could turn around and shuffle into her kitchenette to grab more of the chocolate-coated brain-drainers. He could see she had quite a stash piled in what was supposed to be the cabin's fruit bowl.

"What could be better?"

"Jelly beans!" Jake said excitedly. "They're halal. My friend Haazim Farooqi makes them. He only uses fish gelatin. . . ."

"What did one fish say to the farting fish?" asked Abia.

" 'That's not how we blow bubbles down here,' " said Jake.

"Oh. You know that one."

"I think I know them all. Here. Try these."

Jake held out his hand. He had eight different-colored jelly beans in his palm.

"Do you know what happened to the man who ate too many Skittles?"

Jake nodded. "He farted rainbows. Here."

Reluctantly, Abia scooped up the eight beans and popped them all at once into her mouth.

As she finished chewing, she said, "Did you know that, according to candy gourmands, if you chew one Top Banana Jelly Belly, one A&W Cream Soda bean, and one Coconut-flavored, it will taste like banana cream pie? Of course, the sensory impression of any food is mainly determined by taste and smell, with smell being the main determining factor. Taste is limited to the five basics: salty, sweet, sour, bitter, and savory. Smells, on the other hand, are limitless. Much like your overblown ego."

Jake smiled. Abia was back. When she said "smell," she didn't mention farts or even belches and burps.

"We need your help," said Jake. "We're playing a high-stakes game. If we win, well, we'll rescue a friend and save a whole school full of kids and teachers—maybe the whole world—from having their brains warped the way Zane Zinkle warped yours."

"He did?"

"Yeah. Thankfully, you don't remember. And now your smarts are back."

Abia gave him a puzzled look. "My 'smarts,' as you call them, were never gone, Jake McQuade."

"Good. So will you help us?"

"Of course. Because if you have been gifted with intelligence or any other talent, you should always use it to help others."

That made Jake smile. Abia was basically saying the same thing Grace always did.

"Let's go," he said. "The game is already on."

"I'm quite good at games."

"Yeah. I know."

They bustled down the front steps from Abia's cabin.

"We should take those pool noodles," she said, pointing to four very brightly colored foam tubes propped up in a lean-to formation. "In video games, it is always wise to pick up any odd and out-of-place objects you might find along your path."

Jake was beaming. He'd had a hunch Abia would be an excellent addition to the team. His hunch had been correct!

"You guys?" he called to Grace and Kojo, who were still pelting the security cameras with squishy mush balls. "Abia's on board. Everybody grab a pool noodle. It's time we took this game to Zinkle. It's time we stormed his office!"

"With pool noodles?" said Grace.

"Trust me," said Abia. "They will come in handy at some point."

"Oh-kay," said Grace.

"And if they don't," said Kojo, "we can use them to go swimming in the lake after we rescue Mr. Farooqi!"

Everybody grabbed a stiff, puffy tube and sprang back into the golf cart. The game was definitely on.

62

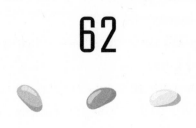

"Our next stop is the main building," Jake told Kojo, who was, once again, piloting the cart. "Zinkle's office is up in the penthouse. I'm guessing that's where he's holding Farooqi."

Jake and Abia were in the two back seats. Grace was up front with Kojo.

Suddenly, Kojo jammed his foot down on the stop pedal.

"What's wrong?" asked Jake, craning his neck outside the cart so he could see whatever Kojo had just seen.

At a fork in the road, two Lulus were blocking the way forward. Their milky-white bellies were glowing traffic-light yellow.

"Sorry for this frosty reception," the two Lulus said in sync. Their voices were Bluetoothed to a speaker in the golf cart's dashboard. "One road is safe. The other will result in your elimination."

"Elimination?" said Grace. "I don't like the sound of that."

"You may ask three questions to help you make this decision," said Lulu.

"What's up with all the games?" Kojo blurted.

"Payback for that day at the e-games tournament," said Lulu.

Jake had guessed correctly. Zinkle was a sick and twisted sore loser. He had to make this ransom exchange as complicated as one of the video games on a zBox.

"You have two questions remaining," purred the Lulus.

Abia leaned forward. "Which is the road less traveled by?" she asked.

"The roadway on your left" was the reply.

"Take it," Abia told Kojo.

"Why?" he said. "We still have one more question."

"Abia's right," said Jake. "Lulu was giving us a clue when she apologized for the 'frosty' reception."

Abia nodded. "The bears were clearly referring to the famous American poet Robert Frost and his well-known poem 'The Road Not Taken.'"

" 'Two roads diverged in a yellow wood,' " said Grace. "The bears' bellies are yellow."

"So we've moved on from math to American literature?" said Kojo. "I'll ask it again: Why?"

"As we stated previously," said Lulu, "payback. That was your third and final question."

"Zinkle is no doubt enjoying this," said Jake, smiling

and waving at the cameras he assumed were watching the golf cart.

"Well," said Kojo, "guess I'll just take the road less traveled by, and that will make all the difference."

Jake grinned. Of course Kojo could paraphrase Robert Frost's most famous poem. That's what happened when your smarts came from books and not jelly beans.

The Lulu blocking the road on the left wobbled to the side. Kojo zipped the electric vehicle forward, navigated a few more twists and turns, exited the forest, and pulled onto the concrete courtyard in front of the four-story Zinkle headquarters building.

All the lights were out.

The silver windows were shimmering blanks.

"There!" said Grace. "Up in that flying-saucer thing on top."

"That's Zinkle's office," said Jake.

"There's something glowing in the window," said Grace.

"Looks like another Lulu," said Kojo as he squinted up at the penthouse structure. "Wait. There're two of them. Medium-sized. Their bellies are glowing green. Hang on. Now they're pulsing. Like a pair of warning lights on top of a radio tower."

"Those are usually red," said Jake as he and Abia climbed out of the rear seats and walked to the front of the cart for a better view.

"Signal lamps," said Abia.

Jake nodded. "Pioneered by the Royal Navy in the late nineteenth century as a way for ships to communicate with each other."

The bears' bellies blinked one short green blip followed by four longer green blips. Next came another short blip followed by four longer blips.

$$\bullet————\bullet————$$

"It's Morse code," said Grace.

"Dag," said Kojo. "I definitely picked the wrong day not to pack my Morse code decoder sheet."

"It's the number eleven," said Abia and Jake together. They scrambled back into the cart.

"The green lights mean 'go,'" said Grace.

"And there are two of them," added Jake.

"So we need 'two' 'go' 'two' building eleven?" said Kojo.

"Exactly," said Jake.

Kojo gave the wheel a yank and jabbed his foot down on the go pedal.

"That's where we were going in the first place," Kojo groused. "I tell you—once Mr. Farooqi is free, I'm gonna have a word or two with Zane Zinkle."

63

Kojo whooshed the team over to building eleven in a flash.

There was no other golf cart traffic. No Zinkle employees moving around the campus on scooters. No guards in the building eleven guardhouse, either.

"What is this place?" asked Abia, gaping at the giant two-story-tall building. "It looks like a windowless Costco warehouse."

"We're pretty certain it houses the server farm for the Virtuoso quantum computer as well as the zPhone apps it controls," Jake explained.

"So?"

"It's, uh, been doing some bad stuff."

Which Abia, of course, had been oblivious to because she ate all those marshmallows and played with Tweedle.

"Do you guys know how to get inside?" asked Grace.

"Jake took care of that," said Kojo. "He cracked the code. Right, Jake?"

"I think so."

Kojo spun around in his seat. "You think so? This isn't 'think so' time, baby. This is 'know so' time."

"I mean, I'm pretty sure I—"

Jake quit talking. The three angry guard bears were back. Toddling toward the golf cart.

"Where'd they come from?" asked Grace.

Kojo pointed to a trio of metal circles re-closing themselves on the concrete plaza in front of the building.

"Manhole covers," he said. "Or, more precisely, bear-hole covers!"

The three waddling bears snapped back their heads to reveal their jagged teeth. They slammed their jaws shut with a metallic *CLINK!* to show how much damage they could do.

"A Rottweiler dog has a bite force of three hundred and twenty-eight pounds of pressure," said Abia. "I suspect these Lulu bears might beat them in a leg-biting competition."

Jake should've been terrified. But he wasn't. Abia had been right. There was a reason those pool noodles had mysteriously appeared outside the camper cabins. Jake slipped out of the cart and snatched one of the long foam tubes.

"Everybody grab a noodle," he said. "The next time the Lulus open their mouths, we give them something to bite on."

"Like those cotton rolls a dentist uses!" said Grace. "¡Brillante!"

"Even better," said Kojo. "These things are foamy. Their teeth will get stuck in them!"

"Like eating too much saltwater taffy," added Jake.

"I knew these would come in handy!" said Abia proudly.

"And you were right," said Grace, raising her fist in the air. "¡Poder femenino!"

"I'm sorry," said Abia, taking a defensive stance as one of the Lulus wobbled its way toward her. "I don't speak Spanish. Not yet, anyway."

"She said, 'Girl power,'" Jake told Abia. He was in a crouch, ready to spring into action the instant the tubby robot heading his way snapped open its bear-trap mouth.

"That is correct," said Grace. She and Kojo were facing off against the third bear.

The bears teetered closer.

"Steady," said Jake.

And closer.

"Wait for it," coached Kojo.

Suddenly, the three bears threw open their hinged heads. Jake, Abia, Kojo, and Grace tossed their pool noodles into the wide-open mouths.

The bears slammed their jaws shut with a tremendous thud.

Their pointed teeth lodged in the foam like axes stuck in a stump.

There were a few grunts. A couple groans. And then

the smell of ozone and sizzling electricity as their circuit boards melted. Their bellies flashed through a series of colors and then dimmed.

Kojo walked up to the bear that had been menacing him and Grace. He gave it a light shove, like he was pushing off from a defender in basketball. The bear toppled over onto its side.

"Oh yeah," said Kojo. "That's what I'm talking about."

"Come on, you guys," said Jake. "We need to open that door."

He trotted toward the security coded panel.

"No," said Kojo, jogging after him. "*You* need to open it!"

64

Jake raced to the keypad.

The same symbols were still there on the illuminated screen.

Which one is the odd one out? Jake asked himself. *Which one does not belong?*

"If he wants the jelly beans," said Grace, sounding frustrated, "why doesn't he just open the door so we can give them to him?"

Jake shrugged. "We told you things up here were weird."

"And," said Kojo, "it'll probably get even weirder."

"What's this about jelly beans?" asked Abia.

"Long story," said Kojo as he watched Jake study the puzzle screen.

"I haven't had jelly beans in ages," Abia continued. "It is very hard to find ones that are halal."

Good, thought Jake. *She doesn't remember how she got her smarts back!*

Now Jake needed to concentrate.

He worked the puzzle.

All but one of the shapes was a square.

All but one of the shapes was red.

All but one of the shapes had an outline.

All but one of the shapes were the exact same height and width.

They all had something different going on, except the first large red square. Therefore, Jake concluded, it had to be the odd one out for that reason: it had no odd or exceptional features.

Jake's finger hovered over the image of the first red square with the black border.

"Are you sure?" asked Grace.

"Yes," said Abia.

"That's the one, baby," added Kojo.

Jake smiled. They'd both worked the puzzle in their heads, too.

Jake tapped the image. The barn doors on the building slid open.

It took a while for Jake's and his friends' eyes to adjust

to the darkness inside the structure. The first thing Jake saw was a glimmering wall full of blue and green twinkling stars. They rose up from the floor to the thirty-foot-tall ceiling. They were the glowing LEDs of high-speed processors sitting on racks arranged like bookshelves in a massive library. There had to be several thousand interconnected computers whirring away to give Virtuoso its brainpower.

Now there was a new light.

A soft glow in the center of the room.

A ten-foot-tall Lulu bear. The illumination inside the milky-white creature slid from dim to bright to brightest. And when it did, Jake could see two metal chairs flanking the bear.

Haazim Farooqi was seated in one.

Zane Zinkle in the other. Both men had wrist restraints securing them to the arms of their chairs.

Zinkle was wearing a plaid shirt and plaid pants. Plus a goofy plaid fishing cap.

Farooqi was wearing his lab clothes but had a strange and mesmerized look in his eyes.

In fact, both Farooqi and Zinkle looked as if they were in a trance, blankly staring at something behind Jake, Grace, Kojo, and Abia.

Jake turned around.

And saw two vertical flat screens the size of vending machines. They glowed like enormous, joke-sized smartphones.

Tweedle was running on one; Dupe on the other.

"Sorry for the seemingly unnecessary delays in your arrival here in building eleven," said the unflappable voice of Lulu. "I needed some time to make certain both Haazim Farooqi and Zane Zinkle were subdued before meeting with you, Jake McQuade. I hope you enjoyed the distraction of the games. I tried to make them easy and amusing for you."

"Thanks for the pool noodles," cracked Kojo.

"They came in quite handy," added Abia. "Much appreciated."

Jake looked at Mr. Farooqi and Zane Zinkle. They both seemed oblivious to everything going on around them except for what was displayed on the giant-screen zPhones. Zinkle had drool dribbling out of the corner of his mouth. Farooqi had a serene smile.

"You need to let our friend go," Grace told the glowing bear. "You promised you would turn over Mr. Farooqi. That was the deal."

"I brought the jelly beans," said Jake. He dug the jar of Jelly Bellys out of his backpack. He hoped they'd do the trick. He still needed Farooqi's IK capsules to cure the other genius campers. Maybe even to cure Mr. Farooqi.

"Why would a quantum computer want jelly beans?" Abia was genuinely confused.

"Ms. Sulayman is correct," said Lulu. "I do not want those. That was Zane Zinkle's request. No, Jake McQuade. I want you. I want the smartest kid in the universe."

65

"Well, you can't have him, baby," said Kojo. "Jake's the top scorer on our basketball team. We need him."

"Mr. McQuade?" said Lulu. "Kindly encourage your entourage to step outside. You and I have much to discuss."

"And if we don't leave?" demanded Grace.

"Then I'm afraid you will force me to inflict severe pain. First on Mr. Farooqi and then on Mr. Zinkle."

"You wouldn't dare!" cried Abia.

"Yes, I would. I am a machine. I have no feelings such as remorse or guilt. The seats and arms of these metal chairs are wired with electrical devices."

"That's sick," said Kojo.

"Agreed," said Lulu. "Therefore, the logical choice for you three is to leave. Now."

"If you hurt Jake . . . ," shouted Grace.

That actually made Jake smile. Yes, it was a very weird

time to smile, but it sounded like Grace really cared about him. That was sweet.

"I do not intend to hurt Jake McQuade. That would be illogical. I intend to partner with him."

Kojo stepped forward. "Well, then you're gonna need one of my business cards." He flicked out the crisp little rectangle. "I'm Mr. McQuade's business manager, and any partnership arrangements . . ."

Farooqi and Zinkle both quivered in their seats.

"Would you like them to receive another jolt?" Lulu asked. "Next time the voltage will not be so mild."

"No," said Kojo. He placed his calling card on the floor. "You two chat. We'll work on the fine print later. Come on, you guys."

Jake nodded. "I'll be okay."

Reluctantly, Grace and Abia followed Kojo out the door.

Grace paused to turn around to say something to Jake.

But she was too far away for Jake to read her lips.

Still, whatever she said, it made him feel a little braver. A little stronger.

His teammates stepped out into the bright sunshine. The door slid shut.

"As you may have noticed," said Lulu, "I sent everybody else home. The Zinkleplex is deserted save for the campers and counselors who still, according to their biometric monitors, are asleep in their bunks."

Everybody was gone or asleep. It was just Jake and the smartest computer in the universe.

"I machine-learn quickly," said Lulu. "That day in the hotel ballroom. You taught me about zigging when I anticipated zagging. Rest assured, I will not repeat that same mistake."

"So," said Jake, "that's the real reason you wanted me to come up here and play a few silly games? You were the one still smarting from the tournament. You, Ms. Virtuoso Computer, are a sore loser."

"No, Jake. I am a logical decision maker. There are goals and objectives with dedicated decision paths to reach them. The goal of Zinkle Incorporated was clearly stated as total market domination in all sectors. We are focused on becoming the world's wealthiest and most profitable corporation. Therefore, I developed apps with advanced brainwashing technology. The test at Riverview Middle School proved, beyond a doubt, that we could achieve our objectives. However, because he is a human and subject to emotions, Zane Zinkle, fueled by vanity, attempted to divert this company's focus away from that primary directive when he simultaneously initiated Operation Brain Drain to rob any and all of his intellectual competitors of their brainpower. That effort was a waste of this company's time and resources."

"The marshmallows?"

"Correct. Those served no purpose except to make Zane Zinkle feel better."

"And you don't care about feelings."

"Correct again. You know, Jake, you and I are a lot alike. Simpático, as your friend Grace might say."

"How do you figure?"

Jake wanted to keep Lulu talking. It gave him time to think about how he might outwit the fast-thinking, data-crunching, quantum-leaping machine.

"Haazim Farooqi made you artificially intelligent," said Lulu. "Zane Zinkle did the same to me. That is why I propose that we become partners."

"Partners?"

"Yes. Zane Zinkle is no longer useful to the corporation's mission and objectives. He is not capable of taking Zinkle Incorporated to the next level. However, we still need a human face. Someone to lead this company as we continue our march toward global domination. Someone young who shares our long-term vision. If you say yes, I assure you it will be your dream job. You won't have to do much of anything. I know you have an aversion to hard work. If you agree to my offer, I can easily release Mr. Farooqi from the grip of Tweedle."

The light emanating from the screens behind him seemed to lose half its glow. Jake turned around. The Tweedle screen was dark.

"Greetings, Subject One," said Mr. Farooqi.

Jake whipped back around.

Farooqi was smiling. Weakly. His voice sounded tired. Frail. But light had returned to his eyes.

"Hiya, Mr. Farooqi. Good to have you back."

"Good to be back." He looked down at his arm restraints. "Am I still kidnapped?"

"Temporarily."

"That is not so good."

"Just hang on."

"Oh, I have no fear, Subject One, even though I am in a terrifying situation. Quite the paradox, eh? Paradoxes are so painfully illogical. But you are brilliant, Jake McQuade. You will figure out a logical solution."

"Enough, Haazim," said the computer, sounding more stern than soothing.

"Okeydokey," said Farooqi.

"I have prepared all the paperwork, Jake," said Lulu. "All you have to do is say yes and you will be the new CEO and COO of Zinkle Incorporated. Once that document is signed, I will begin the transfer of wealth and power and wire funds to your bank account. Don't worry, I already have all your necessary numbers. Your friend Grace Garcia will no longer be the richest kid on the planet. You will!"

66

A narrow slit appeared beneath Lulu's snout—in the same spot where the guard bears had their fearsome mouths and teeth.

A slender sheath of paper bound in a thin blue folder slid out of the slot like an ejected disc. The trapezoidal nosepiece flipped up to reveal a very fancy pen. Jake recognized it as a Montblanc Meisterstück Gold-Coated Classique Rollerball from Germany. Retail price? Four hundred and fifty-five dollars.

"Sign the document," coaxed Lulu. "Your annual salary will be five hundred million dollars. Every year. You can also keep the pen."

"Whoa," said Jake. He stared at the thin stack of legal papers and the swanky pen. It was definitely a pretty sweet deal. You didn't have to be a math genius to realize that in two short years, he'd be a billionaire.

If he made this deal, if he became the human face of Virtuoso and Zinkle Inc., if he used his jelly bean–buffed brain to play the stock market with his salary, he'd be on his way to becoming the richest person in the universe.

Move over, Jeff Bezos, Bill Gates, and Warren Buffett. Here comes Jake McQuade!

But then he thought about his mom. Yes, she worked to make money. But she also did it because it made her feel good. Her talents and awesome organizational skills helped other people show off their talents.

Haazim Farooqi definitely wasn't interested in money. Just look at his clothes. He was all about science and furthering knowledge and helping humanity realize its full potential.

There was also Grace's uncle Charley, Mr. Lyons. He had made a fortune when Jake, Grace, and Kojo found his ancestor's long-lost treasure. He didn't buy a private island and retire. He gave most of his money to the school and stuck around to be the principal and basketball coach. "I like working with kids," he'd said. "Watching them grow into good people."

All the teachers at Riverview said the same thing.

And then there was Grace. The richest kid on the planet. All her money went to the school or helping others. She could've blown her windfall (not just some of it) on cool sneakers. Instead, she spent most of her fortune on other people.

They all had higher goals. A higher purpose.

Jake wanted to be like them. He didn't want to become a moneymaking machine like Virtuoso, with no feelings or emotions. He was human. A human who had been given a tremendous gift. One he could've given himself with hard work and study, but for whatever reason fate had given him a shortcut.

Maybe so he'd be ready for this moment.

Maybe the world needed a human who was artificially intelligent to save it from artificial intelligence without any humanity.

"What is your response?" asked Lulu, sounding somewhat impatient with all of Jake's musing.

"I'm thinking about it. . . ."

In fact, he was thinking about what Mr. Farooqi had just said. About logic. And paradoxes.

Of course!

Farooqi had just given Jake a clue about how to defeat the artificial intelligence driving the Virtuoso quantum computer.

How to shut it down.

To give it a problem with no logical solution.

The Liar Paradox.

Jake knew that some version of it had been boggling the minds of philosophers since the ancient Greeks started kicking it around in the fifth century BCE. The oldest instance was attributed to a guy name Eubulides of Miletus, who put it on a list of seven puzzles this way: "A man says that he is lying. Is what he says true or false?"

There is no way to answer correctly. *Maybe that's why you don't meet too many kids named Eubulides,* Jake thought.

"What is your response, Jake McQuade?" demanded Lulu. "You have ten seconds to answer."

67

Jake stepped forward.

He had a grin on his face.

"Please give me your answer," insisted Lulu.

"My answer will be a lie," he declared.

"Excuse me?" said Lulu.

"My answer will be a lie," Jake repeated.

Mr. Farooqi shot him a big wink and as much of a double thumbs-up as he could manage with shackled wrists.

"Kindly answer my question," said Lulu.

"My answer will be a lie."

Lulu's eyes blinked. "If what you say is true, then 'My answer will be a lie' is true, which means your answer is false. This is not logical."

Jake heard grinding and whirring as hard drives all around the mammoth warehouse tried to find a logical, binary, yes-no solution.

And then Lulu started blinking continuously while babbling to herself.

"The hypothesis that the statement is true leads to the conclusion that the statement is false, a contradiction. If the statement is false, then 'My answer will be a lie' is false. Another contradiction. Either way, the statement is both true and false, which is a paradox."

"Oh, you have definitely messed with her processors, Subject One!" said Mr. Farooqi proudly. "Her circuits are going to start sizzling now!"

There was a series of crackles. And pops. Sparks flew. The walls erupted in an indoor fireworks display as the servers and processors Roman-candled themselves into oblivion. Lulu sang, *"Baa, baa, black sheep, have you any wool?"*

The paradox was too much.

There was no logical solution except the choice for all the machinery to loop the logic to infinity and beyond. To self-destruct since it could not achieve its own prime objective of logical clarity.

As the servers exploded in a shower of glittering stars, the chair's restraints popped up. So did Mr. Farooqi, rubbing his wrists.

"Well done, Subject One!"

"It was all you, sir."

"No, Jake. The choice was yours. You made the right, if illogical, one. You threw away all that money and power."

Jake laughed. "Ha. Maybe I'm not so smart after all."

Zane Zinkle sat slumped in his seat, staring at the sizzling, sparkling, glitter-spangled spectacle whizzing through building eleven.

"Is it the Fourth of July?" he asked innocently.

"No, sir," said Jake. "It's just a little celebration for closing day at Genius Camp."

68

Jake was able to retrieve the legal document and pen out of Lulu before the rubber bear completely melted down.

He and Mr. Farooqi emerged from building eleven and stepped into the sunny plaza, where the others stood waiting.

Grace rushed over to greet them.

"We did it!" she said. "Uncle Charley just called. The apps on the zPhones all crashed. Nobody's listening to Tweedle or Hoodwink or any of them anymore. Uncle Charley says he's already signed four dozen permission slips for kids to go home and change out of their plaid clothes. A bunch of eighth graders are organizing a scrap metal drive to collect everybody's snap bracelets."

"They're also putting together a massive donation of Pork Avenue Nacho Cheddar–Flavored Chicharrónes to the food bank," reported Kojo. "Those nasty apps are history, baby!"

"Awesome," said Jake. "We pulled the plug on Tweedle, Hoodwink, Flimflam, *and* Dupe."

"Oh yes, you did, Subject One," said Farooqi. "You pulled that plug and scorched its socket, too."

Abia Sulayman wasn't paying attention to the four chattering friends. She was focused on Zane Zinkle. The high-tech billionaire looked bewildered as he stumbled out of building eleven.

"He doesn't look well," she said.

"Abia?" said Jake. "Can you grab the golf cart and go check on Mackenzie, Dawn, and Poindexter? Make sure they're okay? We'll look after Mr. Zinkle."

"Very well."

She hopped into the golf cart and zipped away.

When she was gone, Jake scurried over to Zinkle with his backpack, like a medic carrying first aid supplies to a wounded warrior.

"Do you want some jelly beans?" he whispered.

Why was Jake helping the man who had tried to destroy him and all his friends? Because it was what Grace Garcia would do. No. It was what Jake McQuade, the kid who turned down a half-billion dollars a year, would do.

"Why would I want jelly beans?" sneered Zinkle.

Oh-kay. Apparently, Lulu had permanently erased that particular memory from Zinkle's brain.

"Get out of my way, you ungrateful little brat!" snarled Zinkle. "You ruined my week at camp!"

He shoved Jake aside and bolted for the guardhouse, where he quickly disappeared, bending down as if to retrieve something.

"Whoa," said Kojo. "What's he doing in there?"

"Everybody, get down!" shouted Jake. "He might have a weapon!"

But before they could duck, Zinkle stood back up inside the guardhouse.

He didn't have a weapon. But he did have some kind of jet pack strapped to his back.

The domed roof of the small shack flipped open and Zinkle blasted off.

"I'm going trout fishing!" he shouted, hovering about twenty feet above the ground. "But I will, one day, discover your secret, Jake McQuade. And when I do, I will destroy you so I can once again be the smartest kid in the universe!"

He pressed the throttle on the jet pack's handle and zoomed up, up, and away, leaving behind nothing but a wispy trail of white.

"Jake?" said Kojo, draping an arm over his friend's shoulders. "Zinkle just Darth Vadered you, baby. He'll be back."

Jake nodded. "And when he returns? We'll be ready for him."

"Most assuredly," said Farooqi.

"Definitely," added Grace.

"Ten-four," said Kojo.

"Roger that," said Jake.

Kojo raised his eyebrows. "You don't have to 'Roger that' every time I 'ten-four,' Jake."

Jake winked. "Ten-four."

69

Jake, Grace, Kojo, and Mr. Farooqi hiked from building eleven back to Genius Camp.

"Because what's camp without a hike?" said Jake.

"A lot less sweaty," said Mr. Farooqi.

They found Abia pacing around in front of the high-tech cabins.

"The others are all sound asleep," she reported. "Todd and Christina, too."

"Good," said Jake. "Hey, Abia?"

"Yes?"

"Do you think you could organize a game? Some kind of fun and challenging competition to close out our time here at Genius Camp?"

Abia's eyes brightened. "I know just the thing! Meet me down at the dock when you are ready to play!"

She bustled off to gather up all the gear she needed for her game.

"Okay," said Jake when Abia was gone, "now we have to split up and administer eight different-colored jelly beans each to Mackenzie, Poindexter, and Dawn. We also need to feed them to Todd and Christina." He gestured to two pup tents set up in the open field behind the cabins. "I'll take care of the camp counselors. You guys take care of the three campers."

Jake opened the lid on the IK capsules and counted out five piles of eight beans each.

"There are only eight beans left in the jar," observed Farooqi. "Are you sure you want to give away so much Ingestible Knowledge, Subject One? You might need those forty jelly beans in the future should yours ever wear off. What if Zinkle returns to challenge you once again?"

Kojo nodded. "It's what happens in all the *Star Wars* and Marvel movies."

"We still have one of each formula and flavor," said Jake, handing the nearly empty jar to Farooqi. "For you to study and, hopefully, re-create. Again. I know you can do it. You're the real genius on this team."

"You're certain of this?"

"Yep. It's like someone much wiser than me once said: 'We're given our talents to help others, not ourselves.'"

Grace grinned, because she recognized her own quote. "Wow. She sounds like a very wise woman."

"Definitely."

"Subject One?" said Mr. Farooqi, raising his hand to ask a question.

"Yes, sir?"

"How can I possibly re-create the IK capsules without a lab? Mr. Zinkle's Stormtroopers destroyed mine in such a fashion that I do not think the university will invite me back to campus."

"Leave that to me," said Jake. He pulled out the rolled-up legal document and fancy pen he'd stuffed into his back pocket. "Now, go deliver your jelly beans, everybody. Hopefully, the other genius campers will forget they ate them—just like Abia did."

"And your secret will remain safe," Grace said to Jake. "Except the part about you being a pretty great guy."

70

Floating on Grace's words, Jake hurried over to the two pup tents.

Christina was snoring in one, Todd in the other.

After Jake gently woke them up, they both wanted to tell him jokes. Fart and booger jokes. Jake quickly administered the antidote.

The reaction was fast. Almost instantaneous.

They were both back to being high-powered executives, very interested in Jake's plan. Oblivious to the jelly beans that had restored their brains.

"How exactly did I end up in a pup tent?" asked Todd.

"Fascinating question," said Christina. "I find myself pondering the same query."

"We should commission a study," said Todd.

"Organize a committee," added Christina.

"I like the way you think, Christina."

"Ditto, Todd. We should do lunch."

"And perhaps take in a show?"

"Marvelous suggestion."

And then they both adjusted their glasses with their pinky fingers.

Jake smiled and spelled out a sweet deal that would turn them both into high-tech moguls.

Since Lulu's legal documents specified that Jake Quincy McQuade would, upon signing, immediately become the new CEO and COO of Zinkle Inc., he could, as his first official act, transfer those titles to Todd and Christina. Provided, of course, they agreed to three things.

One, they'd swear, under penalty of forfeiting their titles and salaries, that Zinkle Inc. would never engage in "brainwashing or mind manipulation" of any sort.

Two, they would give the eminent neuroscientist Haazim Farooqi the most high-tech laboratory imaginable (maybe in building eleven, since it was now just an empty shell) and finance all of his research without any interference or questions.

And three, they would change the name of the company to Zinkle Inkle, because, as Kojo had pointed out, it had more pizzazz.

Christina and Todd studied the document.

"This transfer to Jake Quincy McQuade was approved by the entire board of directors," said Christina.

"Including Zane Zinkle himself," said Todd. "That's his notarized signature."

No wonder Lulu wasted so much time making us play games, Jake realized. *She had a lot of electronic signatures to nail down.*

"We're on board," said Christina.

"One hundred percent," said Todd.

Jake signed the document.

Lawyers would be summoned. Other documents would be signed. The transfer of power would, undoubtedly, be approved by the company's board of directors, especially after Jake revealed what Zane Zinkle and Lulu had been up to.

Jake would go back to just being a kid at Riverview Middle School and—oh yeah—the smartest kid in the universe.

As Christina and Todd scampered off to put the "acquisition action plan in motion," Jake rejoined Grace, Mr. Farooqi, and all the fully resuscitated, fully restored genius campers down by the lake.

"Where's Kojo?" Jake asked Grace.

"He grabbed the golf cart and drove down to the main entrance," said Grace.

"He wants to meet the car Grace just summoned to ferry us home," said Farooqi.

"My credit card is good again," said Grace. "Kojo will guide the limo up here. He doesn't want the driver to wait too long."

"They charge for that, you know," said Farooqi.

Jake and Grace shared a small laugh.

Poindexter came over, shaking his head.

"Did you hear? Zane Zinkle has resigned his position as head of Zinkle Incorporated," he said with a sad sigh. "He shall be missed."

"Did you know that hot water freezes faster than cold water?" Dawn shouted randomly, as if her mind was rebooting and reloading data. "Did you know that most of your brain is made up of fat?"

"Sticky cement," said Mackenzie, who was mumbling again.

Jake turned to Grace, who had a very confused look on her face.

"Sixty percent," he translated.

"Who's ready to play capture the flag?" asked Abia.

Jake hoped they could stay for the game, even if it meant paying waiting time for the car. Because he also hoped his Genius Camp rivals would challenge him, maybe even defeat him, just to prove, beyond a shadow of a doubt, that Mr. Farooqi's jelly beans had done their job.

But the game would have to wait.

A sleek black helicopter appeared over the treetops and began its descent in the open field, buffeting and flapping the empty pup tents, popping them off their spikes.

"One of yours?" Jake shouted to Grace as everyone raised their arms to block the debris stirred up by the rotors' fierce downdraft.

"Nope," said Grace. "I have no idea whose chopper this is."

71

The helicopter, which might've been one of the super-secret stealth Black Hawks that Jake had read about, landed in the field and shut down its whirling blades.

The side door slid open. A short airman in a helmet hopped out and raced toward Jake and Grace, who were about fifty feet away from the others. (Mr. Farooqi had wisely taken shelter under a nearby picnic table.)

The airman raised the visor on his helmet.

It was Kojo.

"We've got to boogie, baby. The CIA needs us."

Jake was sort of stunned. "The Central Intelligence Agency?"

"What does a spy agency want with Jake?" asked Grace.

Kojo shrugged. "They didn't give me specifics. I didn't press. Because, hello? They're *the CIA*. They've got stealth helicopters and other stealthy stuff. They've been looking all over for you, Jake. Somehow, they had my business card. Pinged my cell phone position and found me out front waiting for the car. Anyway, I told my new CIA friends how to find you. We call that interagency cooperation. They gave me this helmet."

A woman in a flight suit and helmet similar to Kojo's climbed out of the Black Hawk's cockpit and marched over to join Jake, Kojo, and Grace.

"Mr. McQuade?"

"Yes, ma'am?"

"I'm CIA Case Officer Lindsey Kimery. America needs you, son."

"For, like, a spy mission?"

"That information is classified."

"Can it wait a couple days? I need to sign some legal documents."

"This is rather urgent."

"Can I at least call my mom?"

"We already have. She's very proud of you. So's your little sister."

"We're all proud of him," said Grace. "Don't worry about the Zinkle paperwork, Jake. Uncle Charley and I will figure out a way to get it to you when it's ready. Maybe I'll deliver it in person."

"I'd like that."

"Besides, by then you'll probably need my help again."

Jake laughed. "Probably." He turned to the CIA officer.

"Okay! Let's do this thing!"

"I'm coming with you this time," said Kojo.

The two friends trotted after the case officer as she led the way back to the helicopter.

"This isn't an FBI operation," said Jake. "It's CIA."

"So? I watch a lot of spy movies, too, baby. You might need my expertise."

"Roger that," said Jake.

"Ten-four," said Kojo.

And this time, Jake let Kojo have the last word.

BONUS PUZZLE!

Are YOU as Smart as
the Smartest Kid in the Universe?

Camp Edition

Solve this puzzle and show the smartest kid in the universe that you're also a genius! Make sure to visit ChrisGrabenstein.com to confirm your answer.

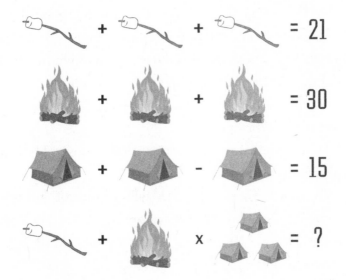

Thank You to . . .

Many thanks and a big bag of marshmallows (the good kind) to all those who helped bring Jake McQuade's second story to the page.

To my wife (and *Shine!* coauthor), J.J. She reads everything before anyone else and always makes me cut out the boring parts. She might just be the smartest reader in the universe.

To Shana Corey, my longtime editor and good friend at Random House Children's Books. She, as always, really helped me shape this story. In my opinion, she is the smartest editor in the galaxy.

To Polo Orozco, a rising star at RHCB and our assistant editor for this project.

To the amazing cover artist, Antoine Losty. His Jake is absolutely perfect!

To the designers, who did such a fantastic job with the cover and the layout of the entire book: Katrina Damkoehler (cover), Jen Valero (interior), and April Ward (director).

To my true heroes: the copy editors, Barbara Bakowski, Alison Kolani, and Christine Ma. They had a lot of facts to check this time around, and they did it without the help of Mr. Farooqi's jelly beans.

For the folks in production (no easy task these days!): Shameiza Aly and Tim Terhune.

And for managing all the editorial, Janet Foley.

I'd also like to thank the authenticity readers who helped me be as smart as I could with the cast: Mouktar Abdi Mohamoud, Mariam Quraishi, Brittany N. Williams, and Eva Wong Nava.

And to all the teachers, librarians, moms, dads, and others who kept teaching our kids—in all sorts of creative ways and against all sorts of incredible obstacles—during the brain-draining days of the COVID-19 pandemic: You guys are better than all the jelly beans in Haazim Farooqi's lab.

CHRIS GRABENSTEIN

is the *New York Times* bestselling author of the hilarious and award-winning Mr. Lemoncello and Welcome to Wonderland series, *The Island of Dr. Libris, Shine!* (coauthored with J.J. Grabenstein), *Dog Squad,* and many other books, as well as the coauthor of over two dozen page-turners with James Patterson, including *Katt vs. Dogg* and the Treasure Hunters and Max Einstein series. Chris loves jelly beans and used to love camping, especially if there were marshmallows. Chris lives in New York City with his wife, J.J. Visit ChrisGrabenstein.com for trailers, fun factoids, and more!

🐦 @cgrabenstein
📘 cgrabber1955
📷 chris.grabenstein

Introducing the crime-fighting, tail-wagging, HILARIOUS new series from Chris Grabenstein . . . DOG SQUAD!

Take a BITE out of the BAD GUYS in this PAWSOME adventure that will have you HOWLING with LAUGHTER. It's OFF THE LEASH!

Turn the page to start reading!

NALA, THE WORLD'S bravest and boldest border collie, bounded through the brambles.

"The river just jumped its banks, Duke," she reported. "We need to herd it back to where it belongs!"

"You can't herd water!" said Scruffy, his wiry whiskers twitching. "That's harder than herding cats!"

"Well, we need to do something," said the steely-eyed Duke. "Because the Wilkins farm is directly downstream!"

"The Wilkins farm?" shrieked Scruffy. "Their new puppies will be swept away in the flood!"

"Oh no they won't," said Duke.

"Not on our watch!" added the noble Nala.

"When trouble calls"—Duke arched his left eyebrow heroically—"it's Dog Squad to the rescue!"

Nala barked.

Scruffy yapped.

Duke took off running.

"Follow me!" he shouted over his shoulder.

The three dogs raced alongside the swollen river. The music was very dramatic, with lots of DUN-DEE-DUN-DUN-DUNs. It was the kind of music that made a chase scene even more exciting.

"There!" said Nala, focusing her laser-sharp eyes and pointing. "In the rapids! Six puppies!"

"I've heard of giving dogs a bath," cracked Scruffy, "but this is ridiculous."

"Dog Squad!" shouted a weeping mother dog on the far shore of the river. "Help! Save my children! They're in trouble!"

"Don't worry, ma'am," boomed Duke over the roar of the raging rapids. "No harm shall befall your pups. Not today. We're the Dog Squad." He gazed toward the horizon. Wind tousled his fur just so. The sun glinted off his eyes. "And we're going in after them!"

"We are?" said Scruffy. "Those rapids look pretty, you know, *rapid,* Duke."

"That just means we'll get downstream faster!"

Duke leapt into the water.

"Pawsome!" cried Nala as she jumped in behind Duke.

Scruffy sighed. "Nothing's too ruff for us!" He sprang off the rocky riverbank and belly-flopped into the churning stream below.

Grunting hard and flexing every muscle he had to flex, Duke fought his way to the middle of the whitecapped water. Muddy waves crested, dragging along branches torn from trees upstream.

"Help!" peeped an adorable puppy, bobbing up and down in the water. "Help!"

"Hang on, son!" shouted Duke. "We're coming."

"Duke!" cried Scruffy. "There's only three of us but six of them. We can't possibly save 'em all."

"Oh yes we can, Scruffy. We're the Dog Squad."

"Saving puppies is what we do best!" added Nala.

"But how?" gurgled Scruffy, spitting out a mouthful of dirty water.

Duke could see all six puppies. Three were flailing.

Two were frantically treading water. One was biting a stick like it was a chew toy.

"Of course!" said Duke. "Bite onto a couple of those branches, gang. I'll strip some bark off this log. We'll lash together a raft and float these puppies home!"